T0083532

foxy aesop

ON THE EDGE

foxy aesop

ON THE EDGE

SUNITI NAMJOSHI

zubaan

ZUBAAN
128 B Shahpur Jat, 1st floor
NEW DELHI 110 049
Email: contact@zubaanbooks.com
Website: www.zubaanbooks.com

First published by Zubaan Publishers Pvt. Ltd 2018
This print edition is not for sale in Australia and New Zealand.
Published in 2018 by Spinifex Press, Australia under the title *Aesop The Fox*.

10 9 8 7 6 5 4 3 2 1

ISBN 978 93 85932 42 7

Zubaan is an independent feminist publishing house based in New Delhi with a strong academic and general list. It was set up as an imprint of India's first feminist publishing house, Kali for Women, and carries forward Kali's tradition of publishing world quality books to high editorial and production standards. Zubaan means tongue, voice, language, speech in Hindustani. Zubaan publishes in the areas of the humanities, social sciences, as well as in fiction, general non-fiction, and books for children and young adults under its Young Zubaan imprint.

Typeset in Garamond 11/15.3 by Sukruti Anah Staneley, New Delhi
Printed and bound at Raj Press, R-3 Inderpuri, New Delhi 110 012

For Alice Eve with my love,
though she is still a baby;
but who, when she is older and knows her Aesop,
might enjoy this account.

contents

acknowledgements
ix

one. BROADCAST YOUR GOOD DEEDS CAREFULLY
01

two. STORIES CAN BE ALTERED TO FIT THE MORAL
12

three. HE PROMISED ME MY LIBERTY AND THEN HE SOLD ME
21

four. IS THAT GLORIOUS?
35

five. WHAT YOU WANT IS WHAT YOU DESERVE
49

six. I LIKE WOMEN
60

seven. SINGING IS ALSO WORK
74

eight. THEY'RE THE SYBIL'S BOOKS READ BACKWARDS
82

nine. SHE CAN DECIDE WHAT HAPPENS NEXT
90

ten. WHAT DOES IT MEAN?
103

eleven. THE DREAM MUTATES AND SHIFTS
118

acknowledgements

The fable about the fish and the heron (*Fish and Fable*) first appeared in *Muse India* Jan-Feb 2014; *Dragonfly Woman* first appeared in *Muse India* May-June 2015, the fable about the fox and the crow (*No Deal*) first appeared in *Weber, The Contemporary West*, Spring/Summer 2016, and the fable about the apple of justice is from *Kaliyug*, an unpublished play co-authored with Gillian Hanscombe.

Further debts include my use of J.C. Stobart's *The Glory That Was Greece*, first published 1911 and later revised for Book Club Associates by R.J. Hopper (4th ed. [1964] 1980) for some background about ancient Greece. I used a range of other sources for details about some of the characters and I confess that I stretched Pythagoras' possible dates (never mind his probable ones) in order to make a meeting between him and Aesop possible. I'm indebted to Professor Laura Gibbs for the website on which I first found Steinhowel's illustrations and for guidance about how to acknowledge the Library of Congress for their use. And as always I'm grateful to Gillian Hanscombe for reading my manuscript.

Aesop labouring beside a stream is thinking up nuggets of common sense and wit. "Why?" I ask him. He doesn't look up. But I want some answers.

"I'm a fellow fabulist," I offer. "The creatures talk when I'm sitting still."

Still no response. I wonder what it feels like to have to be a slave.

"Do you want to be free?" I ask. I know I'm pushing.

"What do you think?"

I push harder. "It's the creatures," I say.

"Yes. They talk among themselves. It's a good noise."

I can only see the back of his head, the hair sparse, some of it greying.

He shows me his face, fierce and brown. Still on his haunches, he stretches out a hand. Co-operation at last? He's willing to talk? And then, without warning, he grabs my wrist.

"Here's your chance. Now you can find out what it was like!"

I can't tell whether he's smiling or snarling. He yanks me in.

one

BROADCAST YOUR
GOOD DEEDS CAREFULLY

I land by the stream somewhere in Samos. He's cleaning pots, scouring them, till they scatter the light like bronze suns. After a while, "Can I help?" I ask, wanting to show willing.

"No," he says. "Now that you're here, you can wait and watch, sometimes you can talk. But you can't impinge."

So I watch. I listen. Perhaps he's thinking of the stork on the far bank or of the fox watching the stork, or of the water hen lurking in the reeds with one eye on the fox and the other on him; but he isn't. He's thinking about chores. I discover that it's only at night when he can't sleep that the stork reappears and talks to him. I can hear what they're saying.

"Had dinner at Fox's yesterday," Stork begins conversationally.

"What, in his own home?" Aesop sounds jealous. It's been a while since anyone has invited him for anything.

"You should have been there! The food was served in an earthenware dish and it smelt heavenly."

"What did it taste like?" inquires Aesop. In his heart he knows that it must have been good.

"'Wonderful!'" replies Stork. "At first I couldn't eat it. My beak kept skidding on the flat plate, but Fox poured the food into a jar – you know, red Samian pottery, with an incised pattern and really rather nice."

"In that case let me be the first to congratulate you on the start of a beautiful friendship." There's a sarcastic edge to his voice, which Stork doesn't notice. "And will you be inviting the fox in return?"

"He's coming tonight!" burbles Stork. "I'm making a crab stew for him."

It's clear the conversation is annoying Aesop. "Will you be serving it in a vase?" he asks.

"Oh no, in a flat dish. I have just the thing," replies Stork.

"Why are you telling me this?" Aesop demands.

"So that you can write about it," Stork answers promptly. "I thought you'd be interested."

"I see," Aesop replies. Of course, he does write about it.

Aesop sleeps. He's brown, not black. I don't think he's African. He's short and sarcastic – like me! I think he comes from the west coast of India. Somebody kidnapped him! Alexander's soldiers! No, not early enough. A trader perhaps? When he's feeling more expansive I'll ask him about it. In the early hours a small figure creeps up to Aesop. It's a middle aged woman. I make noises like the wind howling and that drives her away, or perhaps it was Aesop's snoring. Perhaps I shouldn't have done that? After all, it's not my business. Next time I won't. Next time I might go elsewhere. It might be good to be somewhat discreet. And anyway, it's not his private life I'm interested in.

The days go by. Aesop slaves. I watch. One day a young slave called Androcles tells him that he, Androcles, has been promoted. He's to work in the house. No more heavy duties for him, at least not outside.

"What did you do to please the Master? Or was it the Mistress?" asks Aesop slyly.

"I think it might be because I can play the flute and have a pleasing voice," replies the young man, smiling diffidently. "I'm not sure. It could have just been the Master's whim. Who knows? If I please them, one day I might be free."

Aesop knows perfectly well what it was: it was the young man's appearance, his winning smile, his blue eyes, his blond hair, and the fact that he gave the Master a good massage. For a while Aesop doesn't say anything, then he mutters, "Well, good luck with it," and continues chopping wood, heating water, sweeping the courtyard, clearing the leaves and doing the rest of the day's chores. At least he hasn't been sent to work in the fields. I can see he's disturbed.

That evening, just before mealtime, when he has a few minutes, he peers at himself in a puddle. He mutters, "What if I had a good voice? What if I could sing? Would I be free?"

One of the slaves, a woman called Arachne,

overhears him. (I think it's the same one who crept up at night.) "You!" she laughs. "You're as black as a crow and as sly as a fox! Who do you think you'll ever please?" He's not black, he's brown. It's just that he doesn't get a chance to bathe often. Perhaps he would clean up quite nicely.

Aesop doesn't bother to answer the woman, but that night he makes up a fable about a crow who thought he had a singing voice and a fox who wanted a piece of cheese. The next day he tells it to his Master. The Master is amused, and Aesop too is booted upwards. When Androcles sees him, he asks Aesop how he got there. Aesop tells him the whole story.

"Does your story have a moral?" asks Androcles.

"Yes," replies Aesop. "*If you can't get your supper by singing for it, try using your native god-given wit.*"

"What about, "*Flattery will get you everywhere?*"" offers the young man.

"That too," agrees Aesop.

I intervene. After all, I'm allowed to talk once in a while. "And here's a third. *Sing with your mouth open. Eat with your mouth shut. And only do one or the other at any given time.*"

The two of them laugh. They go about their duties. In their spare time they think about how they might gain their liberty.

🍇

At night Aesop sleeps on the bare floor with a dirty sheet to cover him. They might at least have given him a mattress. But he'd probably refuse – less to carry around, less to put away. In the dark his limbs ache. He curls himself up like a wizened nut. That's how peanuts must sleep inside their shells. He can hear the frogs talking. They're not talking to him. They're complaining about the excess of rain or the lack of it, the width of the pond or the narrowness of it, the mismanagement of weeds, the behaviour of tadpoles and, in short, the miseries and mishaps that govern their lives. They croak and complain all night long. They enter his dreams, so that in his dreams he becomes Zeus. He gives them King Hog and he gives them King Log. Nothing contents them. They

keep on croaking. At last, in desperation, he gives them a King Who Is An Eater Up of Frogs. And then, for the rest of the night, he sleeps in peace.

🍇

Aesops's Master has made a pot of money and wants to be regarded as something more than just another rich man. He thinks a reputation for wit would sit well on him. So every now and then he makes Aesop tell him a story. These stories he passes off as his own when he and his friends are gathered together for one of their feasts. Aesop gets his hopes up. I caution him, "What goes up has to come down."

"What are you talking about?" he asks crossly.

"Gravity," I reply.

"What's gravity?"

"That which keeps your feet firmly on the ground."

"Like a tree?" he sneers. "Be quiet. Let me sleep."

Well, why shouldn't he have his aspirations? He knows the story of Icarus. It's the kind of tale he'd have made up if someone else hadn't done it already. A cautionary tale? Why not? Those who are powerless should be cautious. So then, is that what all his morals amount to: "Be careful"? That's what I want to know about, isn't it? His morals?

Aesop is quite careful, but one night the Master comes home in a wine-fuelled rage and beats him senseless. I can't intervene, and even if I could, what could I do? Aesop finds out the next day that his Master's friends hadn't liked one of his stories – something about a rich man who attracted thieves as a honey pot attracts flies. It turns out they didn't like being called honey pots – it implied they were pot-bellied, which they are, but they don't like it said. Even if Aesop had been careful, how could he possibly have guessed that a reference to honey pots might annoy the rich?

The next morning when the Master begins to fulminate again, instead of shutting up, Aesop tries to explain that it's all right to be a honey pot. He's only saved from another beating because Androcles pleads for him.

Nobody understands why the Master is so partial to Androcles. One evening when the slaves are all gossiping over a meagre lunch, I drop in the word 'blackmail' just to see what reaction it produces. "Not blackmail. Just the reverse!" Arachne tells everyone in her cracked voice. (She's called Arachne because she lives among spiders, and she's the Mistress favourite whipping boy. When the Mistress feels like yelling at someone, she yells at Arachne. She doesn't usually hit her though. She's the one who has a soft spot for Aesop, if you can call it that.) We all want to know what Arachne knows.

"It seems," she tells us, "that the Master was accused of taking some money he wasn't supposed to take. Androcles was present and so he was questioned. He swore that nothing had happened, and because he'd sworn it, he couldn't be forsworn."

"Well," asks Aesop leaning forward. "What did Androcles ask as a reward?"

"Nothing," says Androcles, rolling up. "Nothing at all. Why should I ask for anything for telling the truth? By the way, I'm to be given my liberty in a day or two."

We're astounded, flabbergasted, dumbfounded. I don't really care. I don't impinge and nothing impinges. But the story! What are its implications? What does it mean? '*Virtue is its own reward?*' Virtue certainly has been rewarded. But 'Virtue Rewarded' is a title, not a moral. Perhaps it's a matter of how carefully you broadcast your good deeds. '*Broadcast your good deeds carefully; you never know when they'll sprout.*'

"Is not telling tales on the Master a good deed? *Honesty is the best policy!* Perhaps that is the moral? Is that the moral of all your tales? Not just *Be cautious*, but *Be politic?*" I ask Aesop. Aesop growls and for the rest of the day he doesn't speak to me. That night Aesop has a dream about Androcles taking a thorn out of a lion's paw. He writes it down, but doesn't put in the moral. Says it's self-evident.

Because I want to find out a bit more about him, I challenge him, "You've never seen a lion in your life!"

"I don't need to see one to write about one," Aesop retorts. "And anyway, I have so seen them."

We sound like schoolchildren, but I'm getting somewhere.

"You haven't."

"I have."

"Where?"

"In the Gir Forest!" The answer slips out of him before he can stop himself.

"That's not in Africa."

"Never said it was."

"So you're not an African."

"Never said I was."

"Well, what are you then?"

"None of your business!"

So much for school talk. He tells me to be quiet. He says, "You are, after all, only a figment of my imagination, hauled in from the future."

"And you and your fables," I retort, "are only a

figment of everybody else's imagination. Nobody knows who you really were."

Aesop snores. I think about things. In the fable about the fox and the crow, the fox wasn't honest. As Androcles pointed out, a little flattery can go a long way, and a judicious lie can be extraordinarily pleasing. Perhaps the real moral is '*Honesty can be the best policy; but a judicious lie often works?* Besides how do we know Androcles wasn't lying? Perhaps the Master did take a bribe? Perhaps what Androcles should be applauded for is his loyalty? Or his good sense? Or his prudence? This is not an easy world to survive in. Which world is? Was?

two

STORIES CAN BE ALTERED
TO FIT THE MORAL

The next morning Androcles greets us with a cheerful smile. Aesop and I both wish he wouldn't be quite so cheerful so much of the time. "Come on," he says to Aesop. "We've got the day off. The Master's sending me to inspect his vineyards. He said I could take you. I told him you were good at arithmetic."

Instead of being pleased, Aesop frowns. "How far is it?"

"Oh, it's not far. Half a day to get there and another half day to get back."

It dawns on me that Aesop limps. I point this out to Androcles. "Who are you?" he asks me. Aesop tells him that I'm a figment from the future.

"She thinks she can rewrite my fables," he adds scornfully.

"No, not rewrite," I explain patiently. "Just write new ones, some of which might be based on yours."

"Have you written any about me?" Androcles asks shyly.

"No, not yet." I mean this to sound like a mild threat, but he just smiles happily. Doesn't anything bother him?

In the end Aesop decides to go with Androcles, but I have a feeling it's going to be hard on him. They wrap up some bread laced with garlic and we set off at once. We should have started earlier. It's hot already. But what's that to me? I'm impervious. And if Aesop's suffering, that's too bad. He shouldn't have been so rude about what I write. We trudge along. No conversation. I can see Aesop is concentrating on putting one foot in front of the other. We stop under an old olive tree, or rather, Androcles stops. Aesop has decided he's an automaton – not that he knows about automatons.

Androcles says, "Why don't you rest here for a while? I'll go ahead and get things started. I'll meet you at the vineyard."

I don't think he's showing off, he just means to be kind. Aesop says nothing, and Androcles skips off. Happy clappy Androcles. '*Better to be lucky than to be clever.*' I can hear Aesop thinking. Perhaps he'll make up a fable about that?

Androcles is already well out of sight. Aesop is about to start marching again, when a trader comes along with a pair of donkeys. Their panniers are empty. He must have sold everything he took to market.

"Want a ride, old man?" the trader calls out.

Aesop hates being called 'old man'. He secretly believes that if only he were allowed a good bath and some decent clothes he'd be, if not good looking, at least presentable.

"Can't pay you," Aesop mumbles.

"There must be something you can do to pay your way." The driver's voice is persuasive. I think he feels sorry for Aesop.

"He can tell stories," I say loudly. Well, I can talk. I'm allowed to intervene once in a while.

"Hop on," the trader says, pointing to a donkey. We amble along. Aesop tells him the story of the tortoise and the hare. The driver gets the point and makes the donkeys hurry. We get to the vineyard long before Androcles. He doesn't even know we've been racing. He's just pleased that Aesop got a ride. *Blessed are the innocent for they will never know when they are beaten.* Perhaps Aesop's moral is better? Simpler? Clearer? What was his moral? *Haste makes waste?* No. *Slow and steady wins the race?* But Androcles was going steadily enough. Surely fast and steady would be most effective? Better to be lucky than able? It doesn't matter. Stories can be altered to fit the moral.

"Yes, and morals can be altered to fit the story," Aesop chips in. I hadn't realised I'd spoken aloud. Aesop's in a good mood. He and Androcles share their lunch. They stink of garlic, but I don't mind. I quite like garlic and anyway they're my friends – after a fashion.

Androcles counts the wine jars quickly and Aesop checks the accounts even more quickly. They decide that the Master will be pleased if we take back a few jars. "He'll be even more pleased if we take back a lot," I tell them. "And you might be able to keep a jar or two back."

They like the idea. Androcles goes in search of the man with the donkeys, while Aesop fiddles the accounts. There's nothing in it for me obviously. I can't drink the wine. I don't know why I'm worrying about Aesop's foot. I've noticed that he hobbles when he thinks no one is looking.

The donkey man turns up with several more donkeys. He wants to be paid with three jars of wine. "Xanthus of Samos can afford it," he says. So that's the Master's name. That's what I'll call him from now on. Who wants to call him 'Master'! Meanwhile, Aesop haggles and settles for two jars of wine. The trader agrees, but asks Aesop if he would throw in a story, and if at all possible could the story be about him?

We set off and Aesop begins. "There was once a man who had two donkeys. They were good sturdy beasts and did their work well, but their master wasn't sure he was getting all he could out of them. When he was in a good mood he would pat them and praise them, but when he was in a bad mood he would beat them mercilessly."

"If this story is about me," the trader protests, "you're not being fair. I'm a good master. Ask anyone."

"Unless your donkeys are called Aesop and Androcles, it's not about you, so be quiet," I tell the trader. He shuts up.

Aesop gives me a dirty look. He continues in the present tense without noticing he has changed tense. "One night, after they've been beaten particularly badly, the two donkeys decide to run away. It's a moonlit night. They break down the barn door and run into the fields. Their master hears the noise and chases them. 'Stop!' he yells. 'Where are you going?'

"'We're making a bid for freedom,' the donkeys cry.

"'Don't be stupid. In this world and in this century, donkeys can't be free.'

"'Well, we'll get a better master, who won't beat us quite so mercilessly,' the donkeys tell him. The master promises he'll never beat them so hard again, so the donkeys return."

"Then what happens?" asks the trader.

"Then the three of them live happily."

"And what's the moral?"

"The moral is that *a good master treats his slaves reasonably*."

The trader subsides, but Androcles pipes up. "What about the slaves, I mean the donkeys? What do they learn?"

"They learn," I tell him, "*that politics is the art of the possible.*"

"You mean freedom is possible only if it's possible to be free?" asks Androcles.

"Something like that. Ask Aesop. It's his story." But Aesop is suddenly in a bad mood and won't say anything.

Once we're back we keep three jars of wine, two that Aesop has accounted for and one extra that we say we had to give to the trader. The Master, I mean Xanthus, seems pleased enough with his jars of wine, but he's awkward and blustering in his manner.

"There's something I have to tell you," he says to Androcles, "but it can wait till tomorrow." Androcles pours Xanthus a little more wine. Xanthus decides to get it over with.

"Look here," he says. "Jadmon has made an offer for you. I don't know why, but he's willing to pay five times what you're worth. I couldn't refuse him. He was very insistent." With that he turns on his heel. Androcles doesn't say anything. What can he say? 'What about the liberty you promised me?' Promises made to slaves are not binding. Androcles is shell-shocked and Aesop and I are furious for him.

I take it out on Aesop. "Well, Aesop," I say bitterly, "and what's the moral of this particular story? *Where there's an imbalance of power there can be no justice?* But you wouldn't go that far, would you? Justice serves the rich and powerful and it's the rich and powerful that you have to serve."

Aesop ignores me and heads straight for the wine. He and Androcles give the other slaves one jar to share and keep two for themselves. They drink all night. I can't eat or drink. I can only watch, and sometimes I can say something. They get into a fight about whether it's better to be a slave if you were born a slave or whether it's more bearable if you've had a few years at least of being your own man. They want to beat up someone; but there's no else, so they swing at each other. The next morning they can barely get up. They have to get up. They've been summoned. Jadmon has arrived.

Androcles the beautiful looks sleazy. He has two black eyes, he's limping and his clothes are filthy. As for Aesop, he never looked like much, but now he looks unfit to appear before anybody. All the attention is focussed on Androcles.

"This is the slave I wanted to buy?" asks Jadmon unbelievingly. "This isn't the same man."

"Oh, it's Androcles all right," Xanthus snarls. "I don't know what has happened to him, but I'll give him such a beating he'll never forget it."

"You said you'd give him his liberty and now you're selling him," Aesop pipes up suddenly. "What do you think has happened to him!"

Wow! Good for Aesop! Where did he get the courage? Xanthus can't believe his ears. A slave answering back?

"I'll beat the shit out of you!" he roars.

"And then you won't be able to sell either of us," Aesop replies.

Before Xanthus can recover from the shock of being spoken to like that, Jadmon, who has been listening intently, intervenes.

"I'll take both of them off your hands for the

price I first offered you for Androcles," he says to Xanthus. "I've brought the money with me. Here it is."

Xanthus can't resist the money. "Well, take them then," he replies. "And you can do the beating instead of me."

They're led away and I follow of course; only Aesop stops and asks if he might collect his things. A slave with belongings? It makes Jadmon raise his eyebrows, but permission is granted. Aesop returns with a bit of parchment. Jadmon observes this, but says nothing. Suddenly Arachne scuttles up. "Take me too!" Aesop ignores her. I find myself wondering whether Aesop is a nice man. Well, even if he wanted to help her, what could he do? We march into the street, Jadmon leading. His slaves shepherd us.

three

HE PROMISED ME MY LIBERTY
AND THEN HE SOLD ME

Jadmon's house is much larger than Xanthus'. It's near the city walls and the air is cleaner and fresher, not that Aesop and Androcles are in any condition to appreciate this. Jadmon instructs his slaves to find a sleeping place for the new slaves. They're to be given clothes and food. Once they've recovered, they're to clean themselves up. He'll find out what they're good for the next day. We're led to a dormitory for male slaves. It smells a little, but it's not too bad. There are rows of little rolls folded up neatly, presumably the bedding for the slaves. Aesop and Androcles are given clean rolls and a bit of space to themselves. They stretch out and do their best to sleep off their hangover. They're past caring what happens to them.

I decide to explore Jadmon's house and follow the slaves. Two of them go upstairs and lead me straight to Jadmon's wife. She is wearing a plain, pleated tunic, nothing fancy. But she is beautiful! We hardly ever saw Xanthus' wife. She was a cipher. She obeyed Xanthus and did her best to avoid responsibility. Aglaia is altogether different. She looks kind and capable. The slaves report to her that the new slaves have been taken care of and are duly dismissed. I stand there a while, gazing at her. I note that her tunic is pinned with a gold brooch, and it too is beautiful. Eventually, I suppose Aesop will fall in love with Aglaia, albeit from a distance. It turns out that Jadmon and Aglaia are a devoted couple. Some of Jadmon's friends criticise him for spending too much time with his wife.

Anyway, I am glad I've met - I mean seen - Aglaia. I look around the house. It's made out of wood and though not spacious, it has room enough. The floors are only stamped earth. Well, why not? I think of the plastered cow dung on the floors of Indian huts. They haven't thought of that. Outside the main hall there are a couple of tethered goats and a pile of dung in a corner. Goats have to be tethered and dung has to be piled up somewhere. I can smell the dung, but the inner courtyard has a fresh smell, perhaps from the sea. The view across the Aegean is breathtaking. I hadn't realized Turkey – Anatolia? – was quite so close. This Jadmon is richer than Xanthus, and he seems to be decent. Perhaps Aesop and Androcles have fallen on their feet.

The next morning they are summoned by Jadmon. "Why were you so rude to Xanthus?" he asks Aesop.

"Because he treated my friend so badly."

"Do slaves understand friendship?" murmurs an associate of Jadmon's.

"We understand it, but can rarely afford it," Aesop replies.

Before the man can get annoyed, Jadmon intervenes.

"And were you also angry on your own account?"

"Yes, he beat me till I fainted," replies Aesop.

"Explain," commands Jadmon.

"Shall I tell you what happened or shall I tell you a story so that you will understand what I think about it?" inquires Aesop.

It's a strange answer, possibly disrespectful. Aesop is pushing his luck. At any moment Jadmon might lose patience and have them sent to the fields.

Jadmon is indulgent. "A story then," he says to Aesop.

"This is Androcles' story," Aesop begins. "A farmer who had a good, willing, obedient horse was so pleased with him that one day he said to the horse, 'You have given me many years of honest service. As a reward, in a day or two I will allow you to rest and to live out your life peacefully.' The horse hadn't expected such good fortune and was happy. But the very next day the farmer was offered two horses in exchange for his one splendid horse by the king, who had heard of the horse's extraordinary merits. It was such a good deal that the farmer accepted it. All talk of being able to graze peacefully was quite forgotten, that is, it was forgotten by the farmer. The horse was heartbroken and changed overnight into an ill-natured beast. No one could do anything with him. The king withdrew his offer and wouldn't have him. The farmer was outraged and was about to beat the horse within an inch of his life, when a kind-hearted merchant bought him." Aesop stops and looks at Jadmon to see if he has understood.

"And what is the moral?" Jadmon asks quizzically.

"*Managing expectations is good business practice?*" offers Aesop.

"And what is the moral from the point of view of the horse?"

"*If you believe a liar, you're bound to be deceived.*"

"I see," says Jadmon. He turns to Androcles.

"What happened?" he asks.

"He promised me my liberty and then he sold me," Androcles blurts out.

Jadmon smiles and says to Aesop. "I enjoyed your story, but sometimes the stark truth is even more telling. I have some business to attend to. Later I will expect to hear your story."

"What shall we do with them?" the other slaves ask Jadmon.

"Let them wash themselves again. Get them better clothes. Then take them to Aglaia. She'll talk to them and find out what they can do to make themselves useful."

Soon the two of them look better than they've ever looked at Xanthus'. They've slept, they've eaten, they've even had a bath and they are wearing really clean clothes. They stand in front of Aglaia looking nervous and respectful.

"What can you do?" she asks.

Before Androcles can answer, Aesop tells her, "He can take thorns out of lions' feet." I don't know what's got into him. Is he trying to impress Aglaia?

"You must be very brave!" Aglaia exclaims.

"No, no, neither bold nor brave," protests Androcles sheepishly. "It was only a lion cub. It had escaped from its master, who was trying to make a living showing it off as a curiosity."

"What happened?" asks Aglaia.

"It ran up to me in the street and held up its paw. So I bent down and looked. There was a thorn in its paw, which I pulled out. But just then, the owner came up and picked up the cub by the scruff of its neck and took it away."

"So you didn't rescue it?"

"I couldn't." Androcles shakes his head ruefully.

"What else can you do?" Aglaia inquires.

Androcles is about to say that he's a willing worker when Aesop interferes yet again.

"He can sing, my lady, and he can also play the flute."

"Oh, that's excellent. And what can you do?" Aglaia asks Aesop.

This time Androcles speaks for Aesop. "He can read and write and do arithmetic. And sometimes he can make up stories that explode in your mind."

Aglaia looks at Aesop and he tells her, "It's true, my lady. I can read and write and understand numbers. If the keeping of accounts were needed, I could do it."

"And these exploding stories?"

"Oh those are only fables, my lady," Aesop replies modestly.

"We shall see. In a few days time some ladies

are coming to visit me. You, Androcles, must sing for them and you, Aesop, must tell a story. If you entertain us well, then entertaining the household shall be your chief duty. Meanwhile, the steward will give you some household tasks."

And with that they are dismissed.

They start sweeping the courtyard as they have been instructed to do. It doesn't feel like drudgery. The winter sun is pleasant and mild. There isn't much dust. Aesop is making up a story in his head about an ant and a grasshopper, when he's summoned by Jadmon.

"I hadn't forgotten, you see," Jadmon says kindly. "You were going to tell me why Xanthus beat you."

"Well, Sir, the crow in its own way is a sleek and presentable bird, but it lacks colour. One day a particular crow decided that he would distinguish himself by turning into a colourful crow. He bullied a small parrot into giving up its plumage and decked himself in bright feathers. Then he began to promenade among his fellow crows. His fellow crows were much impressed, but one day as he was strutting about, it started to rain and the colourful feathers got soaked and fell off. He looked silly and the other crows made fun of him. That made the crow furious. So he found the parrot and beat him up."

Jadmon has been listening intently. "And the moral?"

"Don't parade in borrowed clothes?" Aesop offers.

"No, I mean, what is the moral for the parrot?"

"Damned if you do, and damned if you don't?"

"I see," Jadmon says. "What happened exactly?"

"I told Xanthus a story about pot-bellied honey pots, which he passed off as his own, but his friends didn't like it," Aesop replies.

"Do you mean the story about flies being trapped in the honey spilt from a honey pot?" Jadmon asks. "I've heard it somewhere. Surely Xanthus' friends couldn't have objected to that? Not unless they thought they were being pointed at as flies?"

"No this was a different story, Sir."

"Tell it to me."

"A housewife, who prided herself on her good housekeeping, noticed one day that the honey in her honey pot had gone down quite a lot. She knew that the household hadn't eaten that much. Someone must be dipping into it. And so to catch the thief she set up a row of pot-bellied honey pots, of which only one contained honey.

"'They'll stand there like twelve, sleek burghers,' she said to herself. 'And when the thief looks at them like an uncertain pickpocket trying to decide which one to rob first, I will have time to nab him!' 'Or her,' she added as an afterthought."

Aesop pauses and explains to Jadmon, "Well, that was the problem, Sir. Xanthus' friends thought they were being compared to honey pots. They didn't like it, so they pooh-poohed the story."

"I see." says Jadmon. "Go on."

"So then Xanthus explained that it wasn't his story anyway, which made matters worse. Because then they laughed at him for stealing from me."

Jadmon can't help smiling. "What happened to the honey pots and the honey pot thief?"

"The thief was a fox, Sir, with a very sharp nose. He had no trouble at all finding the pot that was filled with honey. He ate some honey as usual, and before running away he even had time to write the housewife a little note, suggesting that she fill all the pots with honey."

"Cheeky devil. But foxes can't write," Jadmon responds.

"No, Sir, and on the whole, housewives can't read. It's only a story."

"And what is the moral?"

"Don't take the trouble to outfox a fox. Just keep the honey out of reach?"

"How about the shortest distance between two points is a straight line?" Jadmon offers.

"That's very much to the point, Sir. With your permission I will use it," Aesop says instantly.

Jadmon claps him on the back. "You may use it."

Foxy Aesop! Now Jadmon feels clever and that's much better than impressing upon him how very clever Aesop is.

"You're a good chap, Aesop," Jadmon tells him. "Stay with me and take notes when people come to ask for favours. Your comments may be invaluable. If you are straightforward with me, we will do well together. In turn, I promise never to steal your fables!"

Aesop permits himself a small smile. He's doing well. He bows and blends in with the other attendants. Jadmon continues to see people. Aesop takes notes. The day wears on. I can hear a flute somewhere. Androcles practising? Perhaps the two of them will be happy here.

The day arrives when some of the matrons of Samos visit Aglaia. Aesop and Androcles are called to entertain them. Their audience consists of Aglaia herself, her serving women and the matrons of Samos. Xanthus' wife is among them. As soon as she sees Androcles, she says nastily, "I see you've got him singing and dancing."

"No, he's just going to sing," Aglaia replies quietly.

Some of the women are eyeing him. Androcles seems unaware of them. His eyes are on a spot just above Aglaia's head. He sings simply and without self-consciousness. Androcles in the lions' den? Scatheless! He has a pleasing voice and the women are pleased. Then Aesop tells the story of the sour grapes and the women like that too.

But Xanthus' wife objects, "That's one of my husband's fables!"

Aesop gapes at her, then pulls himself together, bows politely and says, "You have a fine ear, Madam. My own poor story is based on his original. In his story the fox builds a ladder and is eating away happily, when the farmer comes up. The fox hears him and spits out a grape, crying out loudly, 'What terrible grapes. In my entire life I have never come across any that were quite so sour!' Upon hearing this, the farmer abandons the grape harvest. As for the fox, he returns again and again and eats his fill from that vineyard." Aesop bows again in the direction of Xanthus' wife. "And the Master told me, Madam, that the moral of the story is that a clever man always succeeds, whereas honest fools must do without."

The matrons of Samos don't quite know what to make of this. They applaud uncertainly. Xanthus' wife is well pleased; she has asserted herself. As for Aglaia, she gives Aesop a long, hard look and tries not to smile.

❦

Aesop and Androcles no longer have to do menial work. They have been promoted to entertainer status, and, in addition, Aesop has to attend on Jadmon. They're doing well. In spite of being slaves, life goes on pleasantly enough. Jadmon and Aglaia are decent people. They don't shout at their slaves, are never brutal and they deal with everyone as fairly as possible. What's more, they even try to be consistently courteous – to everyone! As slave owners go, they're the best!

🍇

One day, when Aglaia happens to have time on her hands, she asks Aesop to tell her a story.

"Any story," she says, "whichever one you feel like telling."

He begins without hesitation. "There was once a beautiful woman. So great was her beauty that whenever she happened to glance at a mirror, the mirror cracked even though it was made of burnished metal. It was no great matter. She and her husband were happily married and loved one another. If they had to do without mirrors, so be it. But gradually her beauty increased. Without in the least intending to, she not only cracked mirrors, she often broke hearts. In order to prevent this, she took to wearing a veil. It was a nuisance, but she put up with it. Then one day her husband bought a set of really good mirrors. They were so good that they didn't crack at all. Even when she looked properly at them, nothing happened. They weren't even scratched. She and her husband were very pleased; they decided she could take off her veil. And as a result a few hearts broke, but most survived."

Aesop stops.

"Is that the end of your story? Does it have a

moral?" Aglaia asks.

Survival of the fittest? Here's Aesop's chance to say something about his feelings, or at least about how he suffers in silence. But he just says, "No, not really. It's a happy ending."

"What about all those broken hearts and cracked mirrors?"

"Well," answers Aesop firmly, "the ones that remained were better mirrors and stouter hearts and that was clearly an improvement."

"It's a very odd story," persists Aglaia. "What is it about?"

Another chance! But he shrugs. "It's just a story."

And that's as close as he comes to declaring his love. Is he being chivalrous in the sixth century B.C.? Or romantic like Cyrano of the long nose? Or perhaps just sensible? I haven't asked – there are limits to pushiness. I don't think the Greeks were romantics. Perhaps for slaves it was different. As for Aglaia, I don't know what she thinks. Is she just puzzled or does she guess? She says nothing and does nothing. She watches him limp away.

four

IS THAT GLORIOUS?

Jadmon and Aglaia have two small children, Chloe and Philemon, aged seven and six. Their parents dote on them. As doted upon children go, they aren't too bad. Sometimes they pester Androcles to sing them a song or beg Aesop to tell them a story. Androcles makes up little rhymes and even plays games with them. Aesop tends to avoid them; but if they manage to corner him, he talks to them.

He's often found looking across the Aegean at the narrow strip of water that separates Samos from Asia Minor.

"Tell us a story! Please, Aesop?" cries Philemon.

"Please, please, please!" begs Chloe.

Aesop turns around. "You have to answer a question first. If you answer well, I will tell you a story."

"Is this a game?" asks Chloe.

"What will you do if we answer badly?" asks Philemon.

But Aesop isn't to be distracted. "Do you agree?"

"Yes. All right." The children sit down cross-legged on the ground and look up at Aesop. He sits down too on a nearby plinth.

"Right," begins Aesop. "Here is the question: what is the function of children?"

"What is 'function'?" asks Philemon.

"He means what are children supposed to do, silly," Chloe tells her brother. She turns to Aesop. "The purpose of children is to have more children?" she asks diffidently. She isn't sure it's the right answer.

I privately think it's a good answer – very Darwinian and way before its time – but Aesop looks disappointed. "Is that all?" he says.

"The function of children," Philemon says confidently, "is to turn into grownups and fight wars and do glorious things."

"What glorious things," demands Aesop, "besides fighting?"

"Oh I don't know," replies the child. "Singing

songs? Telling stories – if they're really good ones? Winning chariot races?"

"Is that what you mean to do?"

"Yes," says Philemon. "Fight battles, kill enemies and then write a glorious poem about how well I did. Or if I haven't got time, I'll get someone else to write it."

"And you, Chloe?"

"Well, me too, I suppose. I want to do glorious things, only I don't think girls…" Her voice trails away.

"Listen," says Aesop. "Instead of killing people, don't you think it would be better to do something good for people?"

"But killing people is good!" interrupts Philemon. "We get their lands and their goats and sheep. We become rich!"

"It wouldn't be good though, if you were the enemy," Chloe points out thoughtfully.

"We've given you lots of answers," Philemon says to Aesop. "Now what about our story?"

But Aesop is demoralised. "So young and so set in their ideas! You tell them a story," he says to me, "while I think."

"Listen," he tells the children. "I'm tired, but my friend here will tell you a story."

"Where is your friend?" asks Chloe looking around.

"Oh, she's invisible, but she can talk all right," Aesop replies.

I can see some goats on the hillside, so I tell them the Norwegian tale of the three goat kids. "Once upon a time, there were three little goats who had eaten up all the grass on their side of the bridge, so they decided to cross over to the other side. But a wicked troll lived under the bridge. As soon as the first goat began to cross the bridge, the troll sprang up and threatened to eat him. 'Oh no,' said the little goat. 'I'm too little. Eat my brother who is about to cross and is much bigger than me.' So the troll let the first goat go. When the second goat kid started to cross, exactly the same thing happened. The goat kid said, 'Eat my brother who will cross the bridge next. He is much, much bigger than me.' So the troll let the second goat go. Now it was the turn of the third goat. He was bigger and stronger than the other two and he knew that the troll wouldn't let him go. He gathered his strength, charged the troll and knocked him off the bridge. Then he crossed the bridge and ate the grass with his two brothers on the other side and they all lived happily."

"I knew it!" shouts Philemon. "I was right all along. We're supposed to fight our enemies and win gloriously!"

"Why was the troll a bad troll?" asks Chloe.

"Because he wanted to eat the goat kids," I tell her.

"What if he was hungry?" protests Chloe. "And anyway, was it all right to tell the troll to eat his brother instead of him? I mean suppose I said, 'Eat Philemon...'?"

"I'm not bigger than you – yet. Anyway, don't argue," Philemon tells his sister. He's feeling much more confident now. "It's your turn," he says to Aesop. "You promised us a story."

"All right," agrees Aesop and begins: "Once upon a time there was a young goat who lived on the west side of the bridge."

"What was his name?" asks Chloe.

"Philemon," Aesop replies and continues. "On the east side of the bridge lived another goat kid."

"He was also called Philemon," I interject hastily.

"One day," Aesop goes on, "they both decided to cross the bridge at the same time. They met in the middle. Neither would give way."

"That would have been cowardly," Philemon puts in.

"But sensible," Chloe adds.

"As it happened," Aesop tells them, "they each took three steps back."

"Whew," says Chloe.

"And then they charged and knocked each other off the bridge." Aesop is implacable. "And that's how they died."

"Well, I suppose it was a good death?" Philemon says uncertainly.

"It was stupid and unnecessary!" cries Chloe. "I don't like your story at all."

"Does it have a moral?" I ask Aesop.

"Yes," he replies. "Try not to hurt anyone, and if at all possible, live and let live."

"Is that glorious?" asks Philemon.

"It is peaceful and it is sensible," Jadmon tells his son gently. He has come up unnoticed and has been listening to the story. He gives Aesop a rueful smile.

The children clamour for their father's attention. Androcles joins them. They make him sing a happy song and sing with him.

🍇

The days go by peacefully. Though technically a slave, Aesop is treated by Jadmon almost as an equal. I think the only reason he doesn't free him is that he doesn't want to lose his company. Androcles too is happy enough. He sings his songs and plays his flute. Aesop makes up stories and thinks of Aglaia sometimes from a vast distance. I wonder whether I should return to my own life. Not much is known about Aesop. Why not leave him here living out his life on the shores of a blue sea? Have I learnt what I came for? The point of his fables? What he's actually saying? Are they cautionary tales, teaching people how to survive? Perhaps there's something more to his stories? I'm not sure I've understood him.

I catch him in his favourite spot staring across the Aegean. He seems to be in a good mood. "Aesop," I say, "if you found a small purse belonging to Jadmon with 50 drachma in it, would you return it to him?"

"Yes," he replies carelessly. He's watching a ship sailing past. Does he want to escape? What is he thinking about?

I persist. "You helped to steal wine from Xanthus. Why are you unwilling to steal from Jadmon? Besides, it wouldn't even be stealing if you merely happened to find the purse…"

"Xanthus was a thug and a bully," Aesop mutters. He's still staring at the ship and not really paying attention to me.

"So that's what morality amounts to? One should deal honestly with the people one likes, but one may steal freely from the people one doesn't?"

Aesop turns around. "Of course not! Why do you use stealing as a test of morality? It's not such a big deal you know."

"So it was all right for Fox to steal the cheese from Crow?"

"It was only a piece of cheese, for god's sake!"

"So stealing cheese is all right, but stealing 50 drachmas isn't?"

"If you don't stop bugging me, I'll beat you up!" he threatens and turns away.

"You can't!" I taunt him. "Now who's a bully and a thug? Don't you care about the unfairness of things? Doesn't justice matter?"

He gives me his attention at last. "It does. But it's not that easy, Sprite. Listen, I'll tell you a story based on one that the old brahmin I worked for told me once."

I don't like being called Sprite, but I don't interrupt. I want to know what he has to say.

"Friends quarrel sometimes," Aesop begins quietly, "and one day the monkey and the crocodile quarrelled bitterly. The monkey was tired and had muttered something about always being the one who brought jamboons for the crocodile. The crocodile was hurt. She said that the monkey had insulted her, and that in future she would do without jamboons."

He pauses to explain what jamboons are. "They're like purple plums. They grow in India." As if I didn't know! But I nod at him and he carries on. "One word led to another, and in the end the two friends weren't on speaking terms. At first they were sustained by injured pride, but they missed each other and began to wish that the quarrel could be ended somehow. The monkey consulted a wise old monkey. She stated her case. She demanded justice. Was there no way that the crocodile could be made to see reason? The old monkey listened, then she gave her an apple and said to her, 'Take this apple to your friend.'

"Now the golden apple dazzled the monkey, and she hesitated; but eventually she did what she had been told to do. The crocodile was overwhelmed. 'It's rare and beautiful. Look how it shines. Let's share it!'

"The monkey was pleased. The two friends cut the apple and ate half each. It was delicious. They felt happy.

"Later the monkey reported to the Wise One. 'That apple worked. The crocodile is now being sensible and kind. What was the apple for? Was it magic?'

"'No, no,' the wise monkey replied. 'Apples are for eating.'

"'But surely that apple was a very special one,'

the monkey persisted. 'Was it the Golden Apple of Justice?'

"The old monkey sighed. 'Apples are apples. They taste good. But as for Justice – that is probably the last thing you need.'"

Having told me his story, he walks away. What is he saying? That Love is better than Justice? That's all very well, but what happens when there's only cruelty? I mull things over. Perhaps I shouldn't have chosen stealing as a sign of morality or the lack of it. After all, it has to do with the way property is distributed in the first place. A slave is property. He'd agree that slavery is wrong. Perhaps that's what I should do – ask him what he thinks is definitely wrong. Not today though. I decide to try Androcles instead.

I find Androcles playing marbles with the children. "Androcles," I say to him, "what do you think is definitely wrong?"

"Wrong with what?" he asks absentmindedly, concentrating on the marble between his fingers. "Is something wrong?" Hopeless trying to talk to Androcles, but I persist.

"Who are you talking to?" Philemon demands.

"The sprite," Chloe tells him. Sprite? I'm not a sprite. Oh well, why not?

"Listen, children," I say to them, "what do you think is a really bad thing to do?"

"Coming into the house with dirty feet?" Philemon offers.

"That's not bad. That's just naughty," Chloe informs him in a superior fashion. She knows she is more grown up. She thinks hard.

"I think killing spiders is bad," she says at last.

"Why?"

"Because it probably hurts them to be squashed. And then they don't live any more. Besides, it's messy."

"Have you ever killed a spider?"

She hesitates. "Once. But I don't think I'll do it again."

"What will you do instead?"

"I'll pick it up carefully and put it down outdoors." An eco-warrior in the sixth century B.C.! Wow.

"What if it came back?" Philemon asks.

"I'd pick it up again and put it outside further away," Chloe replies.

"I think it's all right to kill sometimes," Philemon says thoughtfully. "Some hunting and fishing and fighting is all right."

"Why?"

"Well, for self defence," Androcles says, coming to the boy's rescue.

"You kill fish in self defence?"

"We're playing marbles." Androcles sounds cross. "Do you want to play with us or not?"

"I can't," I reply and go away.

Then I come back. I'm not going to let Androcles get away with not answering me. Luckily Aglaia has called the children in.

I begin, "Listen, Androcles. Do you think Aesop is a great fabulist?"

"Yes."

"And do you think fables generally point to a moral?"

"I suppose so."

"Well, what do you think Aesop teaches?"

Androcles shrugs. "He tells it like it is."

"What do you mean?"

"Well, he shows you what human nature's like and tells a story about it, and then people take from it what they can. The other day Aesop told his story about the fox and the grapes. I overheard some of the ladies talking about it. One of them said, 'Clearly the moral of the story is: *If you can't get what you want, start wanting what you can get.*' To which the other replied, 'And if you can't get that?' And the first one said, *'Start persuading yourself that you didn't really want what you wanted in the first place.'* As for the story that Aesop said Xanthus made up, no one liked that one much except Xanthus' wife."

"They weren't supposed to."

"So you see it all depends."

"On what?"

"On people, I suppose."

"So are you saying that Aesop is such a bad fabulist that people can make his stories mean anything they like?"

"Of course not. Look, Sprite, don't go on at me. I don't always know what to think. I don't know how to make up fables, but I'll tell you something that really happened. You remember Arachne at Xanthus' house? One day, she managed to trap a mouse that had got into the house and was going to boil it to death in hot water – her preferred method of killing mice – but I persuaded her to give me the mouse to take outside and set it free – just as Chloe recommended. Well, the wretched thing came back. So then Arachne spent many sleepless nights trying to catch it again. She was furious with me. 'You are too squeamish,' she said. 'If a thing harms you, you must get rid of it. It's a law of nature.'"

Androcles pauses. "Did she ever catch it?" I ask.

Androcles shakes his head. "I don't know," he says. "I tried not to think about it."

"So that's how you get by? By not thinking about things?"

"I didn't want to think about the poor mouse, because there was nothing I could do. But I did wonder: just because something may be a law of nature, does that make it right?"

"And what did you conclude?"

"I didn't get very far with that either."

I've upset Androcles. Of course, just saying something is a law of nature doesn't make it right! But then what is one supposed to do? Spend one's life ferrying spiders and transporting mice? I'm beginning to think that perhaps I should give up trying to understand. Perhaps Ancient Greece wasn't all that moral? Perhaps I should return to the 21st century? Just as Androcles is about to walk away, Jadmon sends word that young Pythagoras is coming to visit, and he wants us to meet him *en famille*. Now what? Perhaps he'll shed some light?

five

WHAT YOU WANT
IS WHAT YOU DESERVE

The next day Jadmon tells Aesop he's a free man. He even apologizes. "I should have freed you long ago, but I didn't want to lose you."

Aesop doesn't say anything. Just looks at him. It's early in the morning. Jadmon's having breakfast. Aesop is serving him. There's no one else there — except me, of course.

Jadmon looks straight at Aesop. "Sit down," he says. "I would like you to stay on with me, if you would please, as my chief counsellor. You're free now. You don't have to do what I ask. It's a request. I'm also asking Androcles to stay on — as my chief steward. What do you say?"

Aesop looks across at the sea. He says, "I'll stay on for a while if that's all right, but then I want to travel."

Jadmon smiles. "Not a problem. I may want you to travel for me in the near future anyway. Right now we have to prepare for young Pythagoras."

They settle down to discuss the visit. "Tell Pythagoras that in the future his theorem will be the basis of trigonometry," I whisper to Aesop, but he ignores me. He's busy explaining metempsychosis to Jadmon. It's just reincarnation under a different name. Lions. The Gir forest. His brown complexion. I'm not surprised he's familiar with the notion of souls going through different avatars.

They decide that when Pythagoras arrives, he's to meet Aglaia and the children. It's unusual, but Pythagoras has women among his own followers. It's even said that his wife is a philosopher. Jadmon ran into him at the Temple of Hera, they got talking and Jadmon invited him. Simple as that. I don't think they know what a great man Pythagoras is going to be. Well, perhaps Pythagoras knows it. Aesop and Androcles are to be present too. And, of course, I'll be there, though Aesop hasn't introduced me to Jadmon yet. I think he should.

Pythagoras arrives at lunchtime. I expected grey hair, a grey beard. Stupid of me. He's only in his twenties. Jadmon brings him in and he greets Aglaia, nods to Aesop and Androcles in a friendly fashion and smiles at the children. The children aren't sure about smiling back. They've been told to be good, which means they are to be seen and not heard. However, they've also been told that they may ask a question or two if they think it's absolutely essential. They're not sure how they feel about being allowed to meet the clever Pythagoras. Why is he clever? He doesn't look much older than they are. Perhaps it would have been better if they had just been allowed to play outside.

We are served food and wine. Well, they are served. I wonder how Aesop and Androcles feel about being served instead of having to serve. They look comfortable. Aglaia makes sure the children are eating properly and with minimum mess. They talk about Pythagoras' travels in Egypt and even in India with his father as a boy. At some point Aesop tells Pythagoras that one day his great theorem will become the basis of trigonometry. Pythagoras is interested. "How do you know?" he asks.

Now is the time! Aesop should introduce me so that I can take my proper place among these people. I kick Aesop's shins, but, of course, he doesn't feel it. Nevertheless, he does say, "Well, a figment from the future told me so."

"I am not a figment," I inform the company loudly. "I am a person."

"Ah," says Pythagoras knowledgeably, turning in the direction of my voice, "a dislocated soul. I am truly pleased to make your acquaintance. A marvel! And your existence proves beyond doubt the truth of metempsychosis, the wandering of souls!"

He turns to Jadmon, "Why didn't you tell me you had a dislocated soul sojourning with you, Sir? I am truly honoured. You must introduce us."

Jadmon is feeling extremely embarrassed and doesn't know what to say. Luckily for him the children pipe up.

"Oh, her name is Sprite," Philemon tells his father.

"Yes, she's quite nice. Sometimes she tells us stories when Aesop is feeling tired," Chloe adds.

They all look at Aesop. "Er, she's from the future. She yanked herself into our century because she is so interested in us."

Pythagoras is beside himself with excitement. "Of course! It's only logical! Metempsychosis works both forwards and backwards. I suspect that if I tried hard enough I could remember or at least know not only who I have been, but also who I will become!"

"It's not quite like that," I begin gently. Everyone

is listening. I'm the star attraction! I'm enjoying it. "During your travels in India with your father did you never encounter Gautama Buddha, The Enlightened One?"

"I heard of him, but never actually met him," mumbles Pythagoras.

"I saw him once," cries Aesop excitedly, "but was dragged away before I could go nearer." Got him! Why doesn't he want to admit that he comes from India? That can wait.

"At the time of his Enlightenment the Buddha remembered all his past lives, and of course, that was also when he was freed from the cycle of birth and re-birth," I inform the company. "In short, Sir, one remembers one's past lives when one has been liberated; and when one has been liberated, one no longer has any future ones."

Pythagoras doesn't look happy with this, but what do I care? I'm enjoying telling them what's what.

"But surely," says the philosopher. He hesitates. He doesn't quite know how to say that he isn't quite sure whether he has been liberated. I suspect he isn't even sure he wants to be liberated. He thinks he remembers some of his past lives, but probably not all. He tries again, "But surely it might be all right to speculate on what the future might hold?"

Jadmon and Aesop are listening intently. I relent. "There will be poets," I tell Pythagoras, "who will regard these notions from the East as mighty metaphors. So, it can be said, for example, that in your next life, you become what you truly desire. Say your true and secret desire is lecherous and gluttonous, then a lecher and a glutton is what you will become. There's a certain irony in this. You get what you want, and what you want is what you deserve."

There's a silence. Aglaia speaks up. It's uncharacteristic, but she says slowly and thoughtfully, "So then none of us can complain about any suffering, and any dissatisfaction. It is what we have asked for."

"And what we have," says Jadmon regarding his wife and children fondly, "is well deserved."

Aesop and Androcles look uncomfortable. Did they ask to be slaves? They don't say anything.

Philemon, who has only half understood what's been going on, asks his father suddenly, "What was I in my last life, Sir?"

Jadmon ruffles his hair. "You! You young scallywag! You were a tiger!"

"And me? What was I?" asks Chloe.

"You," her father tells her, patting her head and giving her a kiss, "you were a dear, little, sweet bunny rabbit."

"Next time I'm going to be a tiger," Chloe mutters darkly.

"And who do you think you will be next time around, Aesop? Remember we get what we want." Jadmon sounds jovial.

"I think," replies Aesop, "I would like to be a woman. Then I wouldn't have to fight anyone, kill anyone, work for anyone. I could just live at home and look after the children and be protected for the rest of my life."

A look of such scorn flashes from Aglaia's eyes that what she thinks is lit up in neon. THAT'S NOT A WOMAN'S LIFE! She doesn't say anything.

Chloe pipes up. "I've changed my mind. I would like to be an elephant."

"Why?" demands Philemon.

"Because an elephant could throw a tiger over the tree tops!"

"Couldn't!" says Philemon stoutly.

"Could so," replies Chloe.

"Be quiet," commands Jadmon. He turns to Androcles. "What about you? Who would you like to be?"

"I think," says Androcles thoughtfully, "I would like to be a lion – the one I helped. And he could be me if he liked."

"Why?" asks Pythagoras. "A man is so much nobler than a beast."

"I could trot away into the forest. No one would hurt me. I would be king of the beasts…"

"But you would not think great thoughts, or philosophise or be a man held in high esteem," Pythagoras protests.

"I don't think great thoughts anyway," Androcles says amiably.

Pythagoras is troubled. "And you, Aesop, why would you want to be a woman? Jadmon has told me of your great gift as a fabulist. As a woman you would be no one, nothing."

I see Aglaia flinch, but she doesn't interrupt.

"My wife says," murmurs Pythagoras, "that it could be worse to be a woman than a slave. She feels she is also a philosopher, and is always complaining that she is not taken seriously."

"To be a woman and a slave would be worst of all," says Aglaia quietly.

"And no doubt, well deserved!" Aesop interjects sharply. So. He is capable of protest. Perhaps his fables do go beyond mere worldly wisdom?

Jadmon decides it's time to change the subject. He asks Androcles if he would sing for Pythagoras. Androcles scrambles off his couch and stands up to sing. Are guests expected to perform for the Master? Old habits die hard. No harm done though, and Androcles does have a pleasing voice. Besides, I've had my share of being a star at this luncheon. I've managed to stir things up. These people – they may not be homophobic, but they are sexist and they are slave drivers – that's probably worse than being racist.

More food appears. Jadmon calls for more wine. Do the rich eat all day? The children are getting restless. Jadmon excuses them; but when Aglaia rises to accompany them, he signals to her that she should remain. She sits down again, her face expressionless.

After everyone's cup has been refilled, Jadmon says, "We've talked about who we might become. Can we talk a little about who we were?"

"Yes!" I break in enthusiastically. "For example, who was Aesop before he appeared in Xanthus' house? A man of such outstanding ability must have had an astonishing past."

"Be quiet, Sprite!" he snaps at me, but it's too late. They're all looking at Aesop.

He could invent a previous reincarnation, but he thinks that they are interested in who he was before he became a slave. He's right. He begins. "I was born in India. I don't remember my parents. They must have died. I remember crawling about in the servants' quarters, then being sent to do errands and carry messages as soon as I was old enough and reasonably reliable. I was the servants' servant. I wasn't so low caste that I had to do the really filthy jobs. My Master was a king. I never saw him. There were too many ranks between us. The old brahmin who looked after the palace gods co-opted me as his boy-of-all-work. I wasn't high caste enough to be his equal. At least I think that's how it was. He used to recite stories about gods and goddesses and sometimes about animals. I realized that if he forgot how a story went, he just made it up. Sometimes he would delegate me to recite the stories. I did what he did; sometimes I just made them up. Nobody minded." Aesop pauses and drinks his wine. 'Aha,' I think, 'so that's where he learnt his trade.'

Aesop continues. "As a teenager, I was quite good looking –" He stops, embarrassed. "I know I'm not much to look at now, but I was then. I got kidnapped by a pair of thugs who passed themselves off as traders."

"And then what happened?" asks Aglaia gently.

Aesop hesitates. He doesn't want to go on, but she has asked him to. "They used and abused me. We travelled. They taught me to read and write. I kept their accounts in addition to doing other jobs. And eventually they sold me in the Greek markets."

Nobody knows quite what to say. Eventually Pythagoras breaks the silence. "Do you know, I remember being a woman in one of my past lives. I was a courtesan."

Jadmon leans forward. "Like Tiresias, you have been both a man and a woman. What was it like being a woman?"

"I enjoyed myself enormously," says Pythagoras happily. I don't think he cares what he says. He has had a huge amount of wine. "You know, being pleasured by a dozen different men day after day. It was fun."

Aesop and Aglaia glance at each other. They are both appalled. Perhaps women and slaves have something in common? Dependence. Powerlessness. And Fear. Bright Sprite! I knew all that. Didn't have to go to the sixth century B.C. Suddenly I'm cross with myself. What do I want from Aesop? Do I want him to be a hero? Scourge the wicked? Say something harsh in his fables and to the point? I go away to think and let lunch drag to a close.

six

I LIKE WOMEN

Should I ask Aesop about Aglaia? I dislike prying. I am prying, of course. But I dislike prying for no good reason. Are they having an affair? Are they in love? I suppose I could ask him that point blank, but he'd probably frown and maintain a disdainful silence.

I catch him looking across the sea again. What is he looking at across the blue water? Is he homesick for India and a palace in which he was a servant's servant? I clear my throat. "Aesop, do you remember your fable about the lion?"

"Which one?"

"The one in which a lion falls in love with a

beautiful, young woman, and gets emasculated for the sake of love. Her parents say he can only have her if he gives up his teeth and claws. But when he does so and comes to them all toothless and clawless, they throw him out."

"Sure, I remember the fable," Aesop replies quite amiably for him. "I made it up in honour of Androcles, well, in honour of the lion really. It was when Androcles was in danger of falling for someone unsuitable."

"Someone has said – it may not have been you – that the moral of the fable is '*Love can tame the wildest*,'" I tell Aesop. "But I think the moral is – and it is intended solely for the benefit of men, because the assumption is they are the ones who matter – *When dealing with women, retain the upper hand*.'"

Aesop frowns. He's not sure what I'm getting at. He says, "What's wrong with that?"

"It's sexist!" I tell him. "Here's how the story should go. When the lion saw how unwelcome he was and how they had tried to trick him, he informed them that he had only pretended to lose his teeth and claws. They were terrified, but the lion walked away and found himself a lioness whose firm teeth and sharp claws were equal to his own."

"Are you re-writing my fables?" He isn't sure how angry he should be.

"I don't re-write them really. I just use them to make new ones. Your fables are like the Bible or Shakespeare or even Homer. Everyone knows them."

He looks unbelieving, and puzzled.

"Well, if you're using my fables, but not stealing them, I'll be long dead by the time you're doing that." He shrugs.

"What's 'sexist'?" he asks suddenly.

"Reinforcing the view that one sex (usually the male sex) is superior to the other and should therefore retain its power and privileges, including the double standard."

"We are superior," Aesop retorts. "That's just how it is. What's wrong with saying so?"

"Who's 'we'?" I ask him nastily. "I might be a 'sprite' here, but in my other life I'm a woman and a feminist!"

"In a past life I might have been a woman too. So what? I've been promoted. And anyway that lion couldn't have met a lioness who was his equal. The male of the species is swifter and stronger."

"In the wildlife programmes where I come from it's made clear that in a pride of lions it's mostly the females who do the hunting."

"That's because they want to please the lion,"

Aesop retorts.

"Look, if men are superior to women because they are stronger, then it follows that gorillas are superior to men."

"That's silly!"

"Yes, it is silly." We turn away from each other, but I have a parting shot for him. "And I suppose slaves are inferior to their masters and to the wives of their masters because they are less powerful?"

I scoot away quickly before he has time to explode. In a way it's good to be a sprite. They don't see me, so they don't see me as a woman. Heaven knows who they think I am, or whether they even care. I should assert myself.

I could have a chat with Aglaia? After all, she's a fellow woman. And now that we've been introduced, at least she knows who I am, although I'm not sure how a sprite chats with a matron. I barge in on her when she's at her loom.

"Like Penelope?" I say, trying to make conversation.

"Is that the sprite?" she asks. "No, not like Penelope. I don't undo what I've woven. Luckily for me, my husband is with me."

"Who do you think is cleverer?" I demand suddenly. "Jadmon or Aesop?"

"What an odd question! Aesop is a slave. Well, was a slave. Jadmon freed him. Jadmon is his Master. There's no comparison."

"And yet, it's because of Aesop that Jadmon will be remembered."

"What do you mean?"

"Aesop's fables – they'll carry on down the centuries. Everyone will know them. If Jadmon's name lives on, it will only be because he was once Aesop's Master."

The look on Aglaia's face makes it clear she thinks I'm talking nonsense. "What happens down the centuries doesn't matter now," she says comfortably. "Jadmon is a good man and I respect him. He is my husband."

"Aglaia," I ask. "Have you met Xanthus? Do you know of him?"

"I've seen him," she admits. "And I've heard of him."

"If he were your husband, would you respect him?"

"But he isn't," she replies without hesitation, "so it's not a sensible question."

This is hard going. Hypothetical questions are well worth asking; they suggest possibilities. I decide to be blunt. "Aglaia," I ask, "are you content with the status of women in the society you live in?"

"I'm very content with my lot in life," Aglaia answers. "I have a good husband, two dear children, a nice house. I can't answer for other women. Surely it's everybody's duty to be content with what they have? That makes for law and order."

"But don't you want to do something? Think something?"

"I do a great deal," Aglaia retorts indignantly. "I balance the budget. I run the household. I make sure that everyone I'm responsible for is looked after properly. It's a great deal of work and doing it well requires foresight."

"And so you're happy?"

"I try to be," she replies with dignity.

"Look," I say, "you know the story of Penelope, don't you? How, as the suitors pestered her, she did her weaving by day, and her unravelling by night?"

"Of course, she is held up to us as a model of virtue – a good mother and a faithful wife," Aglaia answers.

"While Odysseus frolicked with Nausicaa and Circe and all the rest?"

"Do be sensible, Sprite. You know very well that for men it's different."

"Can't you see that all that weaving and unweaving

is a metaphor for a wasted life?"

"What would you have had her do? Suppose she had taken up with one of the suitors. It would have caused mayhem. The other suitors wouldn't have accepted it, and even if they had, what about her son? He would have lost all his rights."

"She could have ruled in her own right," I point out.

"Well, in a way she did. She kept things going till Odysseus returned. Men don't like to be ruled by women. They would rather have a stupid man than a clever woman. Indeed they would rather have a stupid woman than a clever one! "

I'm gobsmacked. So then she does see. She's perfectly aware of the position of women.

"So you do understand! Then why not try to do something about it?"

"And who would follow me? Why would the men agree to losing their privileges? Why would anyone? And as for the women, why would they risk losing what they have? Do you know Aesop's fable about belling the cat?"

"It's not Aesop's," I mutter. "Some people say it's from the *Panchatantra.*"

"It doesn't matter," Aglaia says impatiently. "Here's how the story would really go if a foolhardy mouse attempted it. The mouse would creep up on the cat while the cat was fast asleep and just as the mouse was trying to tie the bell, the cat would wake up and kill the mouse."

"But at least they'd give the mouse a posthumous medal?"

"Of course not. In a way they'd be glad the mouse was killed. It would justify their own lack of courage."

"So you're saying that men would kill a woman for questioning male supremacy?"

"I am saying that such a woman would pay a heavy price."

"Wow. Underneath it all you are a feminist! Just like me!"

"No, Sprite. Underneath it all, I'm sensible."

"Don't you want things to be different for women? Don't you care about what happens to Chloe?"

"How dare you ask? Of course, I care. But I don't want violence and bloodshed." She relents. "Listen Sprite, I'll tell you a story."

"A fable?"

"Well, it's a story about my mother. After I was married to Jadmon, my mother told me she had petitioned Zeus to grant me children so that she could have a clever and capable grandson and a beautiful granddaughter. I was young then and so I questioned my mother, 'What's wrong with having a clever and capable granddaughter? Why do you want her to be stupid?' 'Oh no,' cried my mother. 'She won't be clever and she won't be stupid. She will be just right – for a woman.' My mother wasn't offering her daughter or her granddaughter much of a choice, but there was no point in arguing so I said nothing. A little later my mother informed me that she had had a dream in which Zeus had said he would grant her wish."

"And so you had Chloe and Philemon exactly as your mother had asked?" I say disingenuously.

Aglaia smiles. "Not exactly," she murmurs. "I ended up with a beautiful boy and a clever daughter. My son will be neither clever nor stupid and for that people will like him. As for my daughter, she is both capable and kind, and the world will be better because of who she is."

I'm silenced. Perhaps Aglaia doesn't need to have her consciousness raised. Perhaps she already knows a thing or two.

"I understand," I say and take my leave.

It's hopeless. How to foment revolution given the odds? Besides, I don't want Aglaia or Chloe to get hurt. And anyway, I'm here to understand Aesop. Is he a contented slave? Surely his status should force him to question the social hierarchy? Most of the time his fables seem to say, "Look, this is how human beings behave." Not all that different from the *Panchatantra* then, which was supposed to instruct princes in the way of the world. Don't fabulists care about changing anything? Criticising anything? Perhaps showing how things are is criticism enough? Isn't that what Swift was doing? "Look, this is what human beings are like – a load of Yahoos!" Who do I want Aesop to be? A philosopher? A revolutionary? A satirist?

And then, surprisingly Aesop comes looking for me. He even calls out, "Sprite, Sprite. Where are you Sprite?" Stupid name, but I answer him.

"What do you want, Aesop?"

"Listen. I think you've misunderstood me. I like women."

"Do you?"

"I think they are lovely. Well, some of them. I admire them."

"Listen, Aesop. Can you make up a fable at will?"

"Sometimes."

"Well, make up one about a woman. Not a young woman, not a beautiful woman, not a rich woman. Just a poor, old woman with nothing much going for her. And don't make her look bad!"

"All right," he says, and takes up the challenge. "A few weeks ago when I was at the Temple of Hera I heard an old woman beseeching the goddess. It was noisy there. Other worshippers were imploring the goddess for whatever they wanted – children, no more children, money, even more money, and so forth. There were street sellers selling fast food, flowers, bribes for the goddess, offerings – whatever the supplicants thought would work. Somehow the cries of the old woman got through to Hera. Perhaps the old woman had a penetrating voice? Who knows. She did not look particularly meritorious.

"'Well, what do you want?' inquired Hera. 'Health? Wealth? Beauty? Whatever it is, I'll give you a little, as you've been going on at me for a very long time.'

"'O glorious goddess, Hera,' the woman replied plopping down on her knees, 'what I would like is a measure of luck.'

"'Granted,' said the goddess. 'From henceforth, whenever you go outdoors, if it is raining, it will stop raining.'

"'I am grateful,' replied the old woman. 'But

please couldn't I be a little luckier than that?'

"The old woman was pushing her luck, but the goddess was patient.

"'Every time you go out, you'll find a few coppers lying on the ground,' the goddess told her.

"'Oh thank you,' cried the woman. 'And might I have one tiny bit more of luck please?'

"'Now what is it?' asked the goddess. She sounded exasperated.'"

Aesop pauses and looks at me. "I nearly intervened to warn the stupid woman, but then thought better of it."

I frown at Aesop for calling the woman 'stupid'.

"What I mean is, irritating goddesses is not a good idea," Aesop explains. He continues, "Anyway, the old woman persisted, 'Could the coppers turn out to be gold please?'

"'Oh, you are a greedy woman!' scolded Hera. 'Just for that I'm taking away the luck I've given you. Instead, when you step out, it will always rain.'

"'Sorry, great goddess,' said the old woman humbly and disappeared into the crowd. But I've heard since that she has done well for herself. She's much in demand as a rainmaker."

In spite of myself, I smile. "And what is the moral?"

"*He who deals with goddesses should keep his wits about*

him."

"But it was an old woman!" I protest. "How about: *She who deals with goddesses should be both careful and clever?*"

"Oh, all right," he says peaceably. "*It's good to be lucky and it's good to be clever. But on the whole it's best to be lucky and clever?* How's that?"

I wonder why he's in such a good mood. Then I realize that Aglaia has come up behind me and has been listening to the story. She too is smiling. Aesop motions to her to sit down. Then he says to me, "Your turn, Sprite. Tell us a story."

Well, why not? They look happy, sitting there together, waiting to be entertained.

"About a woman?" I ask.

"No, about a goddess," Aesop replies glancing at Aglaia.

Hmm. Doesn't he know that women aren't goddesses? I begin, "There was once a woman who was so tired of being bashed and battered, splashed and spattered that she asked the gods to change her into something else. The gods obliged and turned her into a potato."

I pause in order to placate Aesop, who looks as though he is about to protest. "It's all right. I'm getting to the goddess bit."

He subsides and I continue. "For a while the potato woman lived underground. The days passed quietly, though she could not distinguish day from night. No light came through, nobody visited, and though she occasionally heard a passing worm tunnelling through the earth, it was mostly silent and she had nothing to complain of.

"She got bored. She asked the gods to change her please into something more exciting. The gods obliged and turned her into a dragonfly. For a while she was happy, but after an hour or so of hovering about and dazzling everyone in the brilliant sunshine, she realized that dragonflies were extremely short-lived and that very soon she was going to die.

"Once again she petitioned the gods. This time she said she would quite like to be one of them. The gods had seldom come across anyone who was quite so upfront; but the dragonfly woman was persistent, and in the end the gods obliged. And so for a long time the woman went about being a goddess. She tried this and that. She was the goddess of love, the goddess of war, the goddess of fortune, of mercy, of hope, of fear… Eventually she grew tired. 'People keep asking me for things,' she complained. 'Yes, well,' the gods shrugged. 'It goes with the job.' So the woman kept quiet. It was better than being bashed and battered, splashed and spattered and so forth."

I look at Aesop expectantly. "You're a cynical, old thing, Sprite, but it's not a bad story."

So that's all the praise I get? Oh well.

seven

SINGING IS ALSO WORK

Aesop and Aglaia are seeing more of each other because Jadmon has asked Aesop to tutor Philemon. Philemon sits with Aesop for an hour every morning. Chloe is allowed to sit in and sometimes Aglaia joins them. Every now and then Aesop teaches by telling them a story. Today he says to the children, "Do you know the story of the grasshopper and the ant?"

The children nod their heads. "You've told it to us."

"All right, now tell it to me."

Philemon takes the lead. He knows it's his class. "There was once a grasshopper and there was once an ant. They were friends. The ant worked hard all day long and the grasshopper sang. This was good because the grasshopper's singing helped the ant work. But when it was winter the ant wouldn't give the grasshopper anything to eat. She said she had done all the work. And so the grasshopper starved."

Chloe knows she's there on sufferance, but she can't contain herself. "That's not how the story goes," she states categorically.

"Yes, but that's how it might have gone," Philemon retorts.

"You're not allowed to change stories!"

"Yes, you are. Aesop changes them."

"Well, in your story you turn the ant into a mean pig, though she was the one who did all the work."

"She wasn't a pig. She was an ant," Philemon retorts.

In the garden Jadmon and Androcles come into view. Jadmon has his arm across Androcles' shoulder. They are talking. Jadmon looks relaxed. Androcles seems his usual cheerful self. Aglaia watches them, and covertly Aesop watches Aglaia watching them. He looks away and shushes the children.

"Yes, stories can be changed," he says to the children, "but you have to be careful how you change them. They have to mean something."

"Do all stories mean something?" Chloe asks.

Aesop hesitates. I wait for his answer.

"Each time a story is told it means something different," Aesop tells her.

"And each time it's heard," I chip in.

Chloe frowns. "Can't we find a way to make sure that the grasshopper doesn't starve?" she asks.

"He was an unlucky grasshopper," Aesop says gently.

"And she was a hard-hearted ant," Philemon says fiercely.

I feel like showing off. "All right, here's another version of the story," I say to them. "An ant and a grasshopper were excellent friends. They liked and respected each other. The ant admired the grasshopper's musicianship and his easygoing tolerance for the foibles of others. And the grasshopper really liked the ant: her precise movements, her single minded devotion to whatever she was doing and, of course, her appreciation of his talent. It wasn't easy for them to be friends because the ant had no leisure, but they did their best. While the ant worked away, they talked a little. On the whole it was the grasshopper who talked. He told her some of the latest gossip and repeated some of the newest jokes, but mostly he sang. He sang and sang. The days passed pleasantly enough. The other ants were a little envious because the ant seemed to

be enjoying the grasshopper's company. But as she always did her fair share of work, they had nothing to complain about. Winter came and it was time for the ant to return to the anthill.

"'What shall I do?' asked the grasshopper.

"'What do you mean?' inquired the ant.

"'Now that it's winter, I'm likely to starve. I didn't store any food. Can you give me some?'

"'I'll have to ask the other ants,' the ant replied. 'We have a common store.'

"She asked the others and they said, 'No!' indignantly. He hadn't done any of the work. They took the matter to the Ant Queen. Luckily for everyone the Ant Queen was both kind and sensible. She decreed, 'Singing is also work. A certain amount of food should be set aside for the grasshopper every winter, and in summer the grasshopper should sing for everyone.' And so, the grasshopper didn't starve, and when summer came, he sang and sang. He sang for everyone, but most especially for his friend the ant.

"And the moral of the story is: *Fund the Arts!* Or *Artists should be paid for doing their work.*"

I look at the others to see how they liked my story.

Aesop looks mildly interested. Philemon is fidgeting. Chloe says, "I think the moral is: *It's good to have friends.* And in my story, they would take turns – doing the singing and the working." She has a point. Meanwhile, I don't think Aglaia has heard a word of my story. She's looking through the window at Jadmon and Androcles walking arm in arm.

I wonder whether the story about the woman who wanted a bit of luck was about Androcles – the lucky fellow, the golden boy who always falls on his feet? Perhaps it was about Aesop?

The days go by – pleasant days somehow, sunny and slow. I wonder about my relationship to Aesop. What am I doing here? What do I want from him? It's easy enough to corner him these days. He doesn't frown so much. Well, he hardly ever frowns. But I can't ask him, 'What do I want from you?' I have to answer that. I watch him. He's polite to everyone, almost kind. His limp is barely perceptible. And

Aglaia too is subtly different. She was never ungentle, but somehow she seems gentler still. And Jadmon is cheerful. As for Androcles, he was always cheerful.

I corner Aesop, but instead of asking him what's going on, I suddenly blurt out, "What's my relationship to you, Aesop?"

Before he would have frowned, now he just smiles. "Well, let's see. Are you my biographer?"

Boswell to his Johnson? "No!" I reply. "Hardly anything is known about you. I'd have to make you up. And anyway, I'm not interested in you, only in your fables."

"Well, there you are, Sprite." He shrugs.

"And I'm not a sprite!"

"Who are you then?"

"I'm the TPN – the Third Person Narrator! And I have a lot of power," I tell him.

"Would you like to be called Tipon then?"

"No!"

He wanders away in search of Aglaia.

I'm The Tipon. I could easily find out what's going on. I don't have to talk. I could just lurk, be invisible, spy on them. It's possible that I could even control what's going to happen. I've seen it done. But perhaps I'm too enmeshed? Besides I don't want to interfere and I don't want to spy. After all, the four of them don't interfere with each other. But what is my relationship to Aesop? Do I want kinship with him? Am I his big sister? His little sister? I'm not sure I even like him. But then siblings often don't. That would make Aglaia my sister-in-law in spirit so to speak? So what's going on would be my business. I decide to leave them alone.

I pull myself together. I may be The Tipon, but what's physicality to me? I'm disembodied myself. So what Aesop's body endures – the heat and the cold, the indigestion, the pleasure or the lack of it – that's none of my business. Nor his inner feelings? I don't know. I feel confused. A Confused Tipon? Unheard of. I wander away from the house and make my way to Hera's Temple. And that's disconcerting.

I don't get jostled and bumped by the crowds. People just walk through me as though I didn't exist, as though I'm a woman of no consequence – that's too near the bone. And then I stop thinking about myself, because a rumour rushes through the crowd like wind on grass and everyone is disturbed and everyone is murmuring. It's the same phrase: *The Persians are coming! The Persians are coming!*

Even a powerful Tipon couldn't have invented that. The Persians probably are coming. It's to do with history. And even if they can't chop me up or hack me to bits, because I'm just a sprite – has its advantages — I suspect everyone is going to get embroiled. I scoot back to the house and start shouting aloud, "The Persians are coming! The Persians are coming!" Well, they ought to be told. They know already. They're all saying it. If they had modern technology, all the channels would be broadcasting it. It would be spidering all over the internet.

eight

THEY'RE THE SYBIL'S BOOKS
READ BACKWARDS

At home Jadmon summons his Inner Circle, consisting of Aesop, Androcles and Aglaia. I'm not invited, but luckily for him I go anyway. I don't dislike Jadmon. In his way he's a good fellow – not too bright, but not stupid either. He's middle aged, reasonably good-hearted and unlike Xanthus, a decent man. The only thing is he ought to pay more attention to me. He says, "The Persians are coming."

I've thought about it. It's too early. They're not coming, not yet. I tap Aesop on the shoulder to get his attention, but it's no use. And anyway he's busy not looking at Aglaia.

Jadmon glances at Androcles and carries on,

"Some of us met last night to discuss the problems of the city. As you know there are two factions. There's the faction of Syloson, and then there are the rest of us. I think Syloson wants me to join him. His son, Aiakes, has invited me to dine with them, but I'm not sure what to do."

As I said, Jadmon is all right, but he's not cut out for politics. He has inherited his ships and his land, but if he wants to keep all that and hand it on to Philemon and provide a good dowry for Chloe, he'll have to be careful.

"Why don't you want to join Syloson?" Aesop asks.

"He's a bully and a –"

"A tyrant." I interrupt loudly. "And his son, Aiakes, is even worse. And his son Polycrates, will be the worst of all – altogether the most magnificent tyrant. Join their side. They're going to win!"

Jadmon looks around. "Who's that? Is that your sprite, Aesop? Is she a prophet?"

"No, not exactly."

"Command her to speak," Jadmon orders.

"There's to be no commanding around here," I tell Jadmon. "I'm willing to help, but you might say 'please'."

"Please tell us what you know," Aglaia asks.

"I'm from the future, so I only know what you lot have written down. The trouble is some of what you've written may be pure invention. Anyway, one thing is clear – Polycrates rules and ends up being a big deal."

"Do you mean Polycrates, son of Aiakes?" Aglaia asks. "He's only a boy. I know his mother."

"That's the family," I tell Aglaia.

"But they're thugs and pirates," Jadmon protests, "and they're trying to get the rest of us to put money into a new type of ship – triremes would you believe!"

"Yup," I tell him. "That's the way to go. Those ships work. Their naval strength is the basis of their power. And as for piracy – well, it's lucrative."

Jadmon frowns. "How can I be sure you're telling me the truth?"

"I'm not telling you the truth!" I say in exasperation. "I'm telling you what it says in the history books. It's not the same thing."

"Then why should I believe you?"

"Because you don't have anything else to go by, and because sometimes the history books get it more or less right."

"Are these books like the Books of the Sybil?" Androcles asks.

I hesitate and then I say, "They're the Sybil's Books read backwards."

They don't know what to make of this. There's a silence. Aglaia says diffidently, "Dear Sprite, if you could somehow establish that at least one of your prophecies is correct – no matter how trifling it might be. For instance, what are we going to have for lunch? Only I know the answer to that."

"Fish, chickpeas and bread," I reply promptly.

"That's quite correct," Aglaia says.

"But that's not a prophecy. That's an educated guess! I could smell the fish. And anyway, it's what you usually have."

Jadmon tries. "Well, if you have knowledge of some sort, tell me something about myself that only I know. For example, what was my secret name for my favourite horse when I was a boy?"

"Probably Pegasus!" I say sourly.

But Jadmon looks at me wonderingly. "That's right!"

I've had enough. "That too was a guess. For heaven's sake, Jadmon. I don't know anything about you except that you once owned Aesop. You aren't important enough to have gone down in history. You are remembered only because of Aesop."

That was tactless. I try to be careful, but even I

slip sometimes.

"All right, if I matter, tell me something about myself," Aesop demands. "Exactly where was I born?"

"I don't know," I reply. "Nobody knows. You're practically the fictitious author of real fables. It's your fables that matter."

"Very well, which fable am I going to write next?"

"How should I know?" I retort crossly. "According to history hundreds of fables got attributed to you though some of them you know nothing about!" As an afterthought I add, "You're probably going to write the fable about the boy who cried, 'Monster!'"

"I'm not. But I was going to write one about the boy who cried, 'Wolf!'"

"Well, write one instead about the monster. The shepherds didn't believe in monsters and got eaten up!"

We should stop this backchat. Jadmon is still smarting from being told he doesn't matter. Aesop tries to soothe him. "Don't mind her, Sir. She's an ill-tempered sprite, especially when she feels she hasn't been getting due attention. Nevertheless, there may be something in what she says. After all, she is from the future."

I've had enough. "You explain it to him," I say to Aesop.

Aesop looks unsure. "All right, I'll try," he replies. "But you try to explain it to Androcles and Aglaia. It may be important."

"Of course it's important!" I snap back. "Our future depends on it."

Aesop just looks at me. He doesn't spell out the inherent contradiction.

Aglaia, Androcles and I move off to a corner of the courtyard. I try to explain as best I can and they listen to me like good children. There's no ego involved, so they don't bluster. But Aglaia says, "If the future is fixed, then we can't change it." Androcles adds, "And if it's unfixed, then we can't know it." They look pleased – like children who have thought of something clever.

I don't know what to say. "Look, things aren't all that fixed or unfixed. It's a matter of probability. For all I know, depending on what we do, even as we talk the history books are being rewritten."

"I thought you said none of us matter much," Androcles objects.

"All except Aesop. You said he matters," Aglaia puts in.

I don't know whether even Aesop matters to history, but I say to the others, "Well, we've got to try."

That makes sense to them.

And whatever it is that Aesop says to Jadmon works. Perhaps he says the same thing – we've got to try. That evening Jadmon dines at the house of Syloson. Syloson himself is an old man and doesn't join them, but Aiakes is mightily pleased with Jadmon's presents – spices and silk and fine wine. Nor does Jadmon forget a present for young Polycrates – a colt called Pegasus. More to the point, Jadmon has made his allegiance clear while the other aristos are still wondering what to do and which side to be on. For his trouble Aiakes embraces Jadmon and asks if he would undertake a journey to Delphi. He says he has had a dream. According to the dream it is through Jadmon that he will receive the right answer.

After he gets home, Jadmon asks Aesop to summon me.

"Will I bring him the right answer?"

"I don't know," I reply. I've told him already that he isn't important, but it would be wise not to repeat it.

"What is the right answer?" He sounds resigned almost despairing.

"Oh, that's easy," Aesop tells him. "The right answer is that Aiakes and his family will prevail and that will be glorious."

I glance at him. Not like him to be so openly

scornful. What's got into him? And then I have it. He doesn't want to be asked to go to Delphi – for obvious reasons. But what's to be done? There's the march of events. There's the cosying up to Aiakes, there's Aiakes' request. Stuff happens.

nine

SHE CAN DECIDE
WHAT HAPPENS NEXT

Jadmon doesn't want to go to Delphi either. It's a long way away, involves a sea voyage, then a long trek, then the trek back. Along the way anything could happen – dearth, death, discomfort, disease. It's not that Jadmon is a wimp, but he likes his comforts. Besides, what are servants for if you can't ask them to take care of the more unpleasant things in life? He decides to ask Aesop to go for him, forgetting for the moment that Aesop is no longer a slave. Still, Aesop owes him a lot. And anyway, just a trip to Delphi is relatively cheap. Cheaper than building a trireme or fitting out a troop of hoplites. Aiakes could have asked him for much more. Jadmon sleeps on it, and the next day the Inner Circle is summoned again.

This time I'm included, though I haven't been issued a formal invitation. Jadmon tells us about Aiakes wanting him to go to Delphi. "He hasn't actually said I myself have to go. But I do have to ensure that the right answer is brought back."

Before he can ask Aesop to go in his place, I intervene. "It says in some of the books that have come down to the future that Aesop meets his death at Delphi."

Jadmon stares at me or rather at the spot where he thinks I am. "How can you be sure?" he asks. "Are these books correct?"

"I can't be sure," I tell him. "But according to these books, Aesop refuses to give the priests the huge treasure that has been sent with him. And so the priests push him off a cliff."

"Why do I refuse to give them the treasure?" asks Aesop.

"Because you think they are cheating."

"But surely the whole point is to cheat, isn't it? In order to ensure a favourable answer?" Aesop says quite seriously.

"Aiakes didn't mention a large sum of money," Jadmon murmurs. But just then six armed slaves carry in a chest. "Sent by Aiakes to be taken to the priests at Delphi," their leader informs Jadmon. The slaves are told to wait outside, but the chief slave, Herakles, insists that they are to remain with the treasure at all times. We open the chest – stuffed with gold and silver. The slaves then carry the treasure to another room and stand guard over it.

Jadmon now feels that with so much at stake he ought to go himself. But he doesn't want to go. He turns to Aesop. Aesop is unwilling to refuse Jadmon. Besides, he doesn't believe the unreliable books. Books can be foiled. "What's more," he says, "I've got The Tipon on my side."

"Who is The Tipon?" Aglaia asks.

"It's the sprite," Aesop explains. "She is writing this account of me. So she can decide what happens next. It will be all right."

Now I'm in trouble. They're going to blame me for every mess of their own making.

"Wait a minute! There are laws and rules, you know," I interpose.

"What laws?" asks Aesop.

"Action and reaction. Cause and effect," I tell him loftily. "If you do something silly, you have to pay for it."

"What rules?" asks Androcles.

"Verisimilitude and plausibility," I reply gravely.

"For instance I can try to ensure we have fair weather, but I can't make the ship sprout wings and fly."

"So then you're not much help?"

That annoys me. "I think you should treat me with more respect. Of course I can be helpful. For instance I can tell you now that within a week you'll be sailing by moonlight on the bosom of the Aegean."

I meant that to be poetic, but they think it's just moonshine.

There's a silence. Then Jadmon asks, "According to the unreliable books, what happened to the treasure that Aesop refused to hand over?"

"I don't know," I reply baldly. Well, I don't.

We're not sure what to do. Finally we agree that Jadmon should see Aiakes again and ask for more details: how they should travel, in what sort of ship, who should accompany them, what precautions they should take, and, of course, what is the question Aikes wants to ask and what reply would be most gratifying.

Jadmon goes to Aiakes right away and returns quite soon. We gather around. "He wants me to undertake the mission myself. It's too important to entrust to an underling. But he wants me to take Aesop along. He has heard of Aesop's verbal skills and thinks they might be useful."

It looks as though the unreliable books were right: Aesop is headed for Delphi. Perhaps I've contributed to all this? I should have kept my mouth shut about sailing by moonlight on the bosom of the Aegean. Couldn't help showing off. Serves me right. Only I'm not the one who might suffer.

"Has Aiakes said he'll make the arrangements for your journey?" I ask Jadmon.

"Yes. I get safe passage to Athens. His pirates will protect me. And from Athens, horses and a guard to Delphi through friends he has there," Jadmon says dolefully.

"Well, I suppose you and Aesop will have to go," I say. "What would happen if you refused?"

"That's not an option. He made that clear. I'd incur his displeasure."

"And that means?" Androcles asks.

"Loss of ships, loss of lands. I'd like you to come with me," Jadmon says to Androcles.

"Who would look after things here?"

"Aiakes." Jadmon replies promptly. "He has guaranteed that all my ships, all my lands, everything that belongs to me will be safe."

"What about Aglaia and the children?" Aesop asks.

"We'll come too," Aglaia says instantly.

"You can't!" Jadmon is aghast. "Women don't go on voyages."

"I'll dress as a man."

Jadmon splutters. "No! Absolutely not! Who will look after the children?"

Chloe and Philemon have crept in unobserved. "We'll come too," they say simultaneously.

"You can't!" declares Jadmon. "What if you're kidnapped?"

"We'll come as slave children," Chloe offers. "Then no one will want to kidnap us."

Jadmon throws up his hands. Normally he's a mild-mannered man. "No! No! No!" he shouts.

"What is Aiakes offering you for all this trouble?" Aglaia asks gently.

"Some land, two ships and his patronage," Jadmon answers bitterly. "He says the way to rule is by controlling the seas. That's the coming thing. In fact he's giving us space on a trireme going to Athens. He said I could think of it as a kind of luxury voyage."

"Are these triremes safe?" asks Androcles.

"Definitely," I tell him. "According to the books they're a huge success."

"The unreliable books?"

"In this instance, they are reliable."

"It would be useful, wouldn't it," Androcles says wistfully, "if these books of yours were either always right or always wrong. Then at least we'd know where we were."

"What about this book, this so-called account of me, you say you are writing? How reliable is that?" asks Aesop.

"Trust me. For our purposes it's entirely reliable," I inform Aesop.

He isn't sure what to make of this, so he glares at me. We talk a little more. Everyone's anxious to soothe Jadmon. In the end it's decided that Jadmon, Aesop and Androcles are all going and will deal with the Oracle. Aglaia's sister and her husband will stay with Aglaia while we're gone. And as we're going in a trireme our journey should be rapid. No wandering about, no sightseeing. The idea is to return as quickly as possible. I have my misgivings, but don't see what I can do. I wish I'd never said anything about siding with Aiakes. Perhaps things would have taken their course without my saying anything at all. I decide to wait and see and to intervene as and when it's necessary and possible. The Tipon has her limits. 'And I have mine,' I suppose Aesop would say were I to raise the subject.

Even though it's late winter and the seas can be rough, Aiakes wants us to sail the following day. This barely allows Aesop a chance to consult him about what is wanted in the way of an answer and therefore how best to formulate the question. He starts thinking about it right away. I decide that, limited or not, I'm going to make sure Aesop and Aglaia can have a little time together to say goodbye. It's true that Aesop is supposed to be gone only for a short time, but I'm not sure I can bring him back safely. Aglaia looks worried as well. But it turns out that Jadmon feels he ought to spend his last evening with his wife and children. So much for my wishing Aesop and Aglaia well. Still, it's not my business. Or is it? And anyway what choices can I offer them that would bode well? Aglaia to run away with an ex-slave? And what about the children? What about Jadmon? And what would they live on? They know all that. Best to let it go. Think about the voyage.

Jadmon has left Aesop and Androcles to make all the arrangements and take care of details. I try to help. I think about the route. As The Tipon the least I can do is guarantee a pleasant voyage.

Early in the morning, before we set off, Aesop

takes his leave of Aglaia.

"Will you come back?"

"I'll try."

"Will you…?"

"I will."

What can they say? 'Will you remember me?' 'I will. Each time I see a gentle sky I will think of your grey eyes.' There's no point in it, but they mean what they say, barely say.

At last we set off. I have granted us fair winds and favourable weather, though Jadmon gives the credit to Hera. Well, if things go wrong, I hope he gives her the blame as well. I ought to cheer up. This is a voyage. This is an adventure. In a sense it is a quest for knowledge, though I suppose all we're really after is the Sybil's answer, which Aesop, no doubt, is already writing out for her. How much control does anyone have?

*

I come across Androcles staring moodily at the darkening sea. Not like him to worry about things.

"What are you thinking about?"

"I was thinking about the donkey and the bags of salt in Aesop's fable," Androcles answers.

"What about it?"

"I was feeling sorry for the donkey."

"Why? He got away with it twice when the water melted the salt on his back. And if he was unlucky the third time, because the merchant loaded him with sponges, well, being lucky twice and unlucky once isn't too bad."

"Being lucky three times is better," Androcles mutters.

"You identify with the donkey, don't you?"

"Yes. I suppose you identify with the merchant?"

"Why not? I want to try to control what happens."

"So did the poor donkey in its own way."

I look at Androcles.

"What about Aesop? Who do you think he identifies with?" I ask him.

"Oh, he's above and beyond everything. He just tells it like it is," he says morosely.

"I don't think so." Suddenly I feel like confiding in Androcles. "I think a part of him wants to be like you. Listen, I've written a poem about him. I want you to set it to music. I'll read it to you.

Aesop looking at the mute swan
        thinks that her fortune
is better than his: to be beautiful, not ugly
        to fly on two wings
and never to limp, to have as your companion
        a lifelong love
and when death occurs to be able to sing.
        My ramshackle life,
my cobbled whimsies, my tales of so-called
        animal wisdom
are as nothing to this. Of your beauty,

            dear swan, I shall sing

in secret, and of my envy

            never speak."

"What do you think?" I ask. "Do you like it? Can I show it to him?"

"No!" Androcles voice is explosive. "Don't ever show it to him! You would only annoy him. He envies no one, and he doesn't think his fables are 'cobbled whimsies'."

"You don't think he'd like to be handsome like you, beautiful like Aglaia?"

"Perhaps. Sometimes. But it's not important."

"What about Aglaia? Does he care about her?"

"Yes. No. It's not that simple, Sprout."

"Sprite! Not Sprout. No, not Sprite. Never mind. About Aglaia. I thought he worshipped her. I thought it was a grand romance."

"Romance?"

And suddenly I realize that I'm post-romantic. Androcles isn't. Nor Aesop. I try another tack. "Well, do you care about him?"

"Yes. I think I do."

"Why?"

"I don't know why. I admire him. Perhaps being slaves together makes for a bond. Why are you cross-examining me?"

"I'm not. I don't think Aesop likes me much," I mutter thoughtfully.

"It's not that. It's just that you keep hassling him," Androcles replies.

"Hassling him to do what?"

"Be the man you want him to be."

"But I think he's wonderful! Listen. If it's necessary, will you help me to save his life?"

"Of course, I will. Is he really in danger? It's this trip to Delphi, isn't it? I don't think we know what we are doing."

"Did we ever?"

"And that's true too." Suddenly he cheers up.

"This is a voyage of discovery. Something strange and wonderful will happen. We'll learn new things."

I stare at him. He seems as open as daylight. The wind blows through him and the sun lights his hair. "What's your secret?" I ask. "Why are you cheerful? Why does everyone like you?"

He shrugs and smiles. "Because I like them, I suppose? Because I don't expect anything? People aren't all black or white, you know."

"What are they?"

"Brindled!"

"And they like you for seeing them like that?"

"Yes, it comforts them," he says carelessly and goes off in search of Jadmon.

I stare after him. What strange and wonderful things does he think are going to happen? I just see trouble ahead and I don't know how to get out of it.

ten

WHAT DOES IT MEAN?

Perhaps I could have managed it somehow so that Aesop and Aglaia found themselves on the deck of a trireme on a moonlit sea? But that's ridiculous. Completely implausible. And what would I be doing? Trying to give Aesop a little happiness? What about Jadmon? What's he done? Well, he has his Androcles. Or has he? And do I want to know? Besides, there's Aglaia. Ought I not to ask her how she feels? Come to think of it, I did ask her once. She just looked surprised. But that was then. If I started consulting everyone's preferences, time would stand still. The narrative wouldn't move. Nevertheless I ought to deal in the possible and the plausible. And even if

I introduce the utterly impossible, at least in that particular universe it ought to make sense. So then the point of my narrative? *Wish the world well, but watch your back?* And that warning, that too is a kind of wishing well?

I ought not to have been so hard on Aesop. What did I want him to do? 'Strip the ragged follies of the time naked as at their birth'? Hold up the mirror to a species of Yahoo? Make it clear that even a man who has escaped slavery can end up owning slaves himself? A variation on Kafka's man in the ditch? Did I want him to do such a thorough job of showing up our shortcomings that we would never sin again? It can't be done. Our job is to tell the truth as best we can and to entertain. I can see him on the deck working hard at fabricating something. Ah yes, the Question and Answer for the Oracle. The whole thing is fraudulent, but does contain a truth of sorts – Polycrates does prevail.

"What are you doing?" I ask Aesop.

"How does this sound?" he asks in reply. "*Mighty Apollo, god of light and god of the lyre,/ Aiakes begs, to the throne of Samos, might he aspire?*"

"It's in hexameters sort of," I reply doubtfully, "specially if you stress the 'he'. Aiakes might prefer to 'ask' rather than 'beg'. That's the question for Delphi, is it?"

"Yes."

"What's the answer?"

"When wars have been fought and battles won,
When the dust is settled, and all is done,
He who rules shall be Aiakes' son."

"Do you think he'll be happy with that?" I ask Aesop. "He may want to be told that he will rule himself."

Aesop frowns. "Listen, 'son' rhymes with 'won.'"

"It's not in hexameters," I point out.

"It is if you break it up differently."

"But then the rhymes…"

Aesop is now quite cross. "You told me that it was Aiakes' son, Polycrates, that your half reliable, half unreliable books go on about."

"That's true," I reply.

"The prophecy we give him should at least have some possibility of working out. It's something he's going to rely on."

I stop arguing with Aesop. Possibility/ probability – I've been worrying about that too. If I send Aesop to Delphi, am I sending him to his death? The unreliable books say – more than once – that the priests push him over a cliff edge. I need to think. Whatever Aesop's shortcomings as a fabulist, and whatever my shortcomings as a biographer, I don't want Aesop's blood on my interfering hands.

We reach the harbour in Athens just before nightfall the next day. The sailors are amazed. The sea like a mirror, the wind constant – they've never seen anything like it! Never made the journey in such quick time! They give thanks to Athene, to Apollo, to Hera, to whomever they like, to everybody except me. I tell myself I'm allowed one unlikely thing once in a while even if I get no thanks for it. But I wish I had given myself time to think things through. I don't want Aesop to die, not now, not yet, and definitely not because of me.

🍇

We're met at the port by an escort sent by our host, a merchant called Miltiades. As we enter the city I look around: no city walls, a dilapidated theatre in the market place, wooden stands. So this is Athens. Doesn't look like much – not yet, I remind myself, but some day some of the men of Athens will do and say marvellous things. And then I feel a little bit thrilled, and then a little sad because the women didn't stand a chance. I put these thoughts aside. We've arrived. This Miltiades, he doesn't say much, but he takes us into his house, and makes us comfortable. Then over food and wine, he gives us his advice.

"Word will have got about that you have arrived from Samos with a gift for the Oracle. That's useful information for anyone who wants to rob you."

"We have guards," Jadmon says.

"Your guards have been drinking and are sleeping soundly," Miltiades tells him. "My advice is that you leave now for Delphi and travel by night. No one will be expecting you to do that."

"But, but – ," Jadmon is out of his depth and doesn't know what to say. Then he says feebly, "But we were hoping to make the journey by daylight, look at the surrounding countryside." He sounds like a tourist, doesn't understand there is danger. Where there is treasure there is always danger.

"Let's go ahead with the treasure and Jadmon can follow later with the guards," I whisper to Aesop.

"Would it make sense," Aesop asks, "if Androcles and I were to leave for Delphi tonight with the treasure and with whatever guards you can give us, and if Jadmon were to follow later with Aiakes' guards?"

Miltiades looks at Jadmon. "Do you trust them?" he asks bluntly.

"I do, absolutely," Jadmon replies.

"I have mules ready. Let them slip away now with

the treasure and two of my own men," Miltiades tells Jadmon. He turns to Aesop, "When you get to Delphi, go to the Athenian treasury where I have made arrangements for you. Then Jadmon and the guards can arrive at leisure because the treasure will already have got there."

Jadmon doesn't really like the plan, but he hasn't got a better one. So Androcles and Aesop get ready quickly and leave on mule back with Aiakes' treasure. I go with them, of course. We take the back streets and the short cuts, and, as far as I know, we leave unobserved. What am I saying? I am the narrator. We do leave unobserved.

But perhaps we're followed later on? I don't know what I've got myself into. Worst of all I don't know what I've got Aesop into. I thought it was sensible to leave as soon as possible and get the whole thing over with. Am I leading him to his death? No point in discussing it with Aesop. He'll just put me down. But Androcles – he might help. Aesop isn't feeling talkative. He keeps his mule ahead of Androcles. I suspect he's polishing his verses. I glide alongside Androcles and whisper, "Listen, we need to talk."

"Is that you, Sprite?" He smiles. "What do you want to talk about?"

I hate being called Sprite, but this is no time to bother with that. "About Aesop. I think I'm leading him to his death!"

"You want to murder Aesop?" He sounds unbelieving.

"No, of course not. I want to prevent his being murdered."

"Who's going to murder him?"

"The priests at Delphi."

"How do you know?"

"The unreliable books say so."

"But they're unreliable."

"Yes."

"And you're the Tipon."

"Yes."

"You could make something different happen."

"What?"

"We ask the question. We get the right answer. We hand over the treasure. And we all go home and live happily ever after."

"You think that will work?"

"Why not?"

"Because cause and effect don't always work in the way we want them to."

"What do you mean?"

"Shall I tell you a story?"

"Yes." Androcles quite likes stories. "Is it about me?" he asks.

"No, it's about frogs," I tell him. "But it could apply to you if you want it to."

"Go on, then. It will pass the time as we jog along."

"Five frogs, who were friends, were trying hard to pull themselves together and do something. They were tired and hot, and they were also extremely thirsty.

"'This can't go on forever,' one of them said.

"'Yes, it can. It already has, therefore it can. It follows logically,' another one replied. The heat and the dust were making her light-headed. It hadn't rained for weeks. The river was dry, the ponds were only a dent in the ground and the frogs were desperate.

"'We have to do something,' one of them said.

"'What?'

"'Supplicate Zeus.'

"'We've done that for weeks. It hasn't worked,' another replied.

"'Let's do the rain dance one more time,' another suggested.

"'That hasn't worked either,' the first one put in.

"'Well, let's do it again.'

"'No, no. Let's send a petition.'

"'We've sent seventeen!'

"But being stout-hearted frogs they prayed to Zeus, wrote out petitions, collected signatures, and they did the rain dance yet again, and again and again.

"Then one day it rained. The frogs were overjoyed. They danced and they danced. They couldn't help it. The rain made them ecstatic. And then they argued.

"'It was all that praying. We finally got through.'

"'No, no. It was the petitions that did it.'

"'No! It was clearly the rain dance. Haven't you noticed? If we dance enough times, it always rains.'

"'And when it rains, we always dance,' added another frog.

"'So which comes first, the rain or the dance?' asked a philosophical frog.

"'Don't know,' replied a practical one. 'But I'm awfully glad it always works!'"

Androcles looks at me. "So you're not sure you can achieve a happy ending?"

"No."

"And you don't know a rain dance?"

"No."

"Don't worry. Aesop will think of something." Ever the optimist. I hope he's right.

We carry on. It seems to me that this narrative isn't all that simple. It's like a sack with a whole load of wriggling creatures inside it. Not that I'm calling

Aesop a wriggling creature. But it's becoming quite difficult to control his destiny. We travel through the night. We tell anyone who asks that we're traders taking olive oil and wine to the Oracle. They seem to believe us. Once I think we're being followed, but as there are four of us, Aesop, Androcles and two of Miltiades' men – I don't count – whoever it is leaves off. Then just as we are within sight of Delphi we hear horses. It's Jadmon, surrounded by the six guards Aiakes sent to protect the treasure.

It turns out that when the guards woke up and found out that we had left with the treasure, they were deeply unhappy. They insisted on getting horses from Miltiades and chasing after us despite Jadmon's assurances that we were completely reliable. They also required Jadmon to accompany them, though it should have been the other way around. Jadmon should have required them to accompany him. Jadmon didn't protest. After all, when they caught up with us, they would see that we were none of us involved in a plot to run off with the treasure.

I might be the Tipon, but I hadn't anticipated this. On the other hand the reaction of the guards was entirely plausible. Why would they trust two ex-slaves with the treasure? And as for poor Jadmon, from their point of view, he was either a fool or a schemer.

Well, it should be all right. Aiakes' guards will now protect the treasure and once the business with the Oracle is done, we can all go home. They form a ring around us, inspect the treasure and tell Miltiades' men they have been ordered home. Now it's just the guards and us. Jadmon tries to take control.

"Are you satisfied that the treasure is safe?" He addresses their leader, Herakles, a burly fellow with a suspicious frown. "Let us proceed now in an orderly fashion towards Delphi, where we will take lodgings and ask the Oracle for guidance."

The trouble is Herakles doesn't seem to be paying any attention to Jadmon, and the guards are obeying Herakles, not Jadmon. We proceed towards Delphi: Aesop, Jadmon and Androcles are surrounded. I trail along with them. Things don't look good. I am the Tipon, but this is not what I intended.

Suddenly Jadmon tries once again to control what is happening. He rides up to Herakles.

"At least let Androcles return to the house of Miltiades? He can assure him that all is well." Jadmon is a brave man, but he is asking rather than commanding.

Herakles sneers at him. "Militiades' own men can do that satisfactorily. Do you trust an ex-slave? The two of them nearly ran off with the treasure."

"They did nothing of the sort!" Jadmon protests, but Herakles ignores him.

Herakles has been thinking. "Yes, why not?" he says with sudden cunning. "Let Androcles and Aesop both go. And you should go with them as you trust them so much. They'll make sure you are safe. We'll deliver the treasure and come back with the Oracle's answer."

So now he wants to write the narrative? It's clear that he and the other guards are thinking of seizing the treasure.

"You don't even know the question," Jadmon protests. "I have been instructed to deliver the treasure myself to Delphi and to question the Oracle."

"Oh, we'll take care of that," Herakles replies.

Now Aesop intervenes. Whose story is this anyway? Still, if he has a plan, we could use it. I don't want him killed. He whispers to Jadmon who looks uncomfortable with what he's hearing, but he motions Aesop towards Herakles. Before he can speak, Herakles says to Jadmon, "All right, you can stay with us. But tell your ex-slaves to return to Athens. I don't trust them"

"I need to stay with Jadmon," Aesop says. "I have special instructions to do with the Oracle."

"And I'm staying too," Androcles puts in.

They all seem to want to say what's going to happen.

Herakles shrugs and allows Aesop and Androcles to remain with Jadmon. But the discussion has cleared Herakles' brain. His plan has crystallized. He puts Jadmon and the others at the front of the group with two of his men guarding them. The rest who are guarding the treasure are told to go off the road, remove half the treasure and replace it with stones. What they remove, they put into their satchels and rejoin the others unobtrusively.

"Right," says Herakles, addressing Jadmon. "We'll proceed as planned. Only you have to tell the priests you are in a terrible hurry to return to Athens as you've had an urgent message from Aiakes, and so could you consult the Oracle right away, give them the treasure and leave."

Jadmon, Aesop and Androcles glance at each other. Why this change of heart? What is he planning? At last I can interfere. When the guards have moved away a little, I tell them exactly what Herakles has done. "And then," I add, "when the priests find out they've only got half the treasure and come after us, Herakles is going to tell them that Aesop cheated and withheld half the treasure. The priests will get angry. They will seize Aesop and throw him over a cliff, and so fulfil what is written in the unreliable books."

They take this in. They try to think. Aesop grins. "It's all right," he says. "Leave it to me."

At the Temple of Apollo it all goes according to plan. Whose plan? We talk with the priests. Aesop and Jadmon enter the temple. Aesop hands the head priest two pieces of parchment and has a word or two with him. The priestess writhes, and after a few minutes the head priest gives Aesop a piece of parchment. We hand over the treasure or what's left of it and we leave.

Very shortly afterwards the priests of Apollo come after us, accompanied by a party of armed men. They seize Aiakes' guards and take away their satchels. Then the head priest asks, "Which of you is Aesop?"

Jadmon, Aesop and Androcles all point to Herakles, "He is."

"He is to be thrown over a cliff," the head priest pronounces, "for daring to withhold the treasure from us."

"But you have the treasure," Herakles tries to say.

"That is only half the treasure," the priest says smoothly. "Gag him and bind him and throw him over a cliff."

Jadmon, Aesop and Androcles are allowed to leave. And we do leave – as fast as we can.

After a while Jadmon asks, "What happened exactly?"

"Well," says Aesop. "Here's what happened. The high priest kept that part of the treasure that was never found because I was supposed to have withheld it. I was thrown over a cliff, but in name only. And in all this Aiakes' men are barely mentioned. And this way you don't have to ask Aiakes whether his men had instructions from him."

Androcles stares at Aesop. "What does it mean?" he asks.

"If you're looking for morals and meanings, you'll have to ask Sprite here," Aesop says to him.

"It doesn't mean anything," I reply morosely. "Just every man for himself. That's all there is to it."

Aesop won't let it drop. "What about justice? What about injustice? What about fighting for what is right? It was your narrative, Tipon,"

"But all of you ran away with it. At least I managed to save your life."

Aesop grins. "And you expect me to be grateful for letting me live? There's a moral in there somewhere."

I feel that my narrative has been so pulled about that I've lost control. I don't know what to say. I give it a try. "How about, *you might not be able to avoid meeting your Destiny, but you can sometimes sidestep it?*"

eleven

THE DREAM MUTATES AND SHIFTS

We reach Athens. Jadmon has decided to return home immediately, but he's upset when he realizes that Aesop won't be accompanying him.

"You won't come with me?" Jadmon asks for the hundredth time.

Aesop shakes his head. "Remember I'm dead. It's best that way. I'll journey through Egypt, perhaps return to India."

"And you?" Jadmon asks, turning to Androcles.

"I must go with him," Androcles replies.

Jadmon can't hide the hurt in his eyes, but Androcles remains firm, "I must go. He needs looking after."

They say their farewells. Jadmon tries not to look

unhappy. He forgets to say goodbye to me. I don't think he ever realised how important I was. Then he boards the ship and sails away. Gone. As easily as that.

Androcles and Aesop look for another ship. They find one and get ready to leave. They clearly expect to leave me behind. The story is done. I should go home. But I'm not ready to let them go, not quite yet. I follow them on board.

"How are you going to pay for your passage?" I ask.

Androcles pats his pockets. "I kept back a little of the treasure."

"But that's stealing!" I exclaim. "You're supposed to be the good guys."

I shouldn't have said that. That was stupid. But I wasn't expecting it.

Aesop looks weary and slightly reproachful. Androcles says, "Come off it, Sprite. I don't think you or Aesop have the right to say anything to me. You're not good enough!"

"As fabulists?" Aesop sounds surprised.

"No, as people! I'm not saying that you and the Sprite are bad people, but you're not particularly good either. You've done things you ought not to have done. So who are you to judge?"

I don't know what to say. He's right, of course. I

haven't been a particularly good person.

But Aesop says, "That's not the point. I'm a man, not a disembodied fabulist. I want to live, have a good time. The stupidities I've found in human beings, I've found in myself. Don't you understand? I'm like you. My morals are no better than they ought to be. I'm just ordinary, but as a fabulist I'm better than ordinary."

"How can you separate the two? Your story about the fox and the crow – surely the crow couldn't have believed she had a marvellous singing voice." I feel confused.

"But it was such a pleasing thing to believe," Androcles offers. "The best lies are the ones people want to believe."

"So then it should go into a Handbook for Liars?" I know I sound angry, but I don't seem to be able to help myself.

Androcles shrugs. "That's a lesson we learnt as slaves – from our own experience."

I try again. "Perhaps there's another moral," I say diffidently. "Something like: Try not to crave flattery. Try to see clearly."

"Not very catchy," Androcles rejoins.

I glare at him. Then I realise he can't see that I'm glaring, so I say bitterly, "Don't you care about anything?"

But Androcles doesn't want a fight. "I'm not criticizing you," he says peaceably. "Why don't you just accept people as they are? All I'm saying is live and let live, and let the world look after itself."

"It's not looking after itself," I mumble. "It's a mess."

"Look, it's a pleasant morning. The sea's changing colour. Think – think of Aglaia's eyes," he adds with a glance at Aesop. He looks all around him at the sea, at the sky. "Surely all this doesn't make you feel that the world is a mess, does it?"

"No, that's why it has to be saved."

"And you want me to save it?" Aesop asks.

There! That's it. It has been said explicitly. What I want is out of the bag now.

"Yes," I reply defiantly. "You're not really socking it to them. People either think that the fables are just cautionary or that the fables are not about them."

Aesop shrugs. "My fables are as good as the people who read them. I can't even control what happens to my work. How do you expect me to control the world? What can I do?"

"Hold up a mirror so that we're forced to see that the way we carry on really won't do?"

"Has anyone achieved that?"

"There was a man called Swift. He lived a little

more than two thousand years after you."

"What happened to him?"

"After his death for about two hundred years they said he was mad."

"And after that?"

"They turned his most ferocious satire into a children's book."

"There you are, Sprite. Can't change human nature."

"And if you can't change human nature, you can't alter the state of the world," Androcles adds.

"Then why do you write your fables?" I'm practically yelling at Aesop. I didn't mean to sound so passionate, but I want some answers.

"For fun."

This makes me angry. Then I see that he's smiling. He's teasing me. So I say soberly, "Yes, it's true it's fun. It's done for pleasure. But if you had hit harder, if you had somehow managed to change things, I wouldn't be living in a world that's in the same sort of mess as this one."

"Is your world in a mess?" asks Androcles.

"Yes, dearth, death and famine, horrible inequalities, and strutting four-year-olds ruling the nations! Not only that, we're about to destroy the entire planet!"

"What is a planet?" asks Androcles.

"This earth we're living on – it's a round ball. And it spins around the sun," I inform them.

Aesop looks at me reproachfully. "I thought you dealt in the plausible and the probable? Anyway, I don't think we're doing that."

"Doing what?"

"Destroying the earth."

"No, you're not; but we will. Isn't it our job to do something? Say something? Tell the whole damn species to get a grip and grow up somehow?"

"Look, Sprite," Androcles says suddenly pointing at the thrashing sea below. "That's Aesop there, hiding in the waves, pretending to be a dolphin."

I glare at him. "If that's Aesop, then who am I?"

"You're the fox," Androcles tells me thoughtfully, "who couldn't reach the grapes."

"So what am I supposed to do? Pretend that I don't really want the grapes? Tell myself that I want lemons instead? Or declare that the grapes were illusory?" I appeal to Aesop.

For once he takes my side. "Don't mind him, Sprite. Let's have some lunch and we'll make Androcles tell us a story." I don't feel pacified, but I'm curious about what sort of story Androcles might tell.

They settle down to bread and cheese and a glass of red wine. Androcles begins.

"It's about a fox." I glare at him. He continues. "One day Fox said to Stork, 'Look it's no good inviting each other to dinner and then getting cross because you have a long beak and I have a short nose. Let's start over.'"

I interrupt. "And in your story which one of us is Stork, and who is Fox?"

Androcles smiles. "You must decide."

He carries on, "Stork was wary of Fox, but didn't want to seem unfriendly. At last she said, 'What did you have in mind?'

"'Eating doesn't work,' Fox replied. 'We eat different things. Let's just play. For instance, we could run.'

"Fox started running and Stork flapped her wings, but Fox told her it was a running race. And so, Fox ran and Stork tried to run and Fox won.

"'Now, let's have another race,' Stork said to Fox. 'Only this time we both have to fly.' Stork flew and Fox stood still and Stork won.

"'Right,' said Fox. 'And now we have to swim right across the river.' So Fox swam and Stork struggled, and Fox won.

"'And for the next race we'll cross that pond,'

Stork told Fox. She knew it was shallow.

"Fox jumped in and tried to swim, while Stork stepped in and just walked over.

"'Right!' said Fox. 'And now –'

"'No,' said Stork, who had had enough.

"'But I want to prove I'm better than you!' Fox sulked.

"'Oh you are,' Stork replied as she flew away. 'You're a much better fox than I'll ever be!'"

I can't help laughing. "All right," I tell him. "You've made your point. What's more I agree with it. I am a far better fox than you'll ever be!"

Androcles smiles. "It's your turn, Sprite. Now you tell a story – about a fox."

I look at Aesop and he gives me the go ahead, so I begin. "The fox wanted the crow to sing. The crow put her cheese on a branch and told the fox that, as it happened, she was a very good singer with a trained voice and she didn't normally sing for just anybody. He'd have to offer a fee, suggest a time and an appropriate place, and then perhaps she'd think about it.

"'I didn't want to hear you sing, anyway. You probably have an awful voice,' said the fox disgustedly. 'All I wanted was that piece of cheese!'

"'In that case it's a pity you were so rude,' replied

the crow. 'I'm such a rich and successful crow that pieces of cheese come easily to me. I was about to offer you some, but now, of course, I won't.'

"'Oh please,' cried the fox. 'I didn't mean what I said. We foxes are famous for saying we don't want what we do want if we feel we can't have it. Sour grapes and all that. I am, in fact, a great admirer of yours and truly wanted to hear you sing.'

"'In that case,' said the crow nicely, 'I will give you something I'm sure you'll value far more than a piece of cheese.' She scrawled her signature on a large leaf and floated it down to him. Then she flew away with her piece of cheese."

"Why did she scrawl her signature?" asks Androcles.

"Because she was giving him her autograph, of course!" Then I realize that he might not know what an autograph is. "All right, I'll change it so that it makes sense to you. She plucked a small feather from the centre of her breast and floated it down to him. Will that do?"

"Yes, that's much better," Androcles replies. "And of course he didn't want the feather. All he had wanted was that piece of cheese."

"Was it a good story?" I look at Aesop.

"Yes, it was a good story," Aesop replies. High

praise. I can't believe my ears.

It emboldens me. "Now it's your turn. You have to tell a story."

"About a fox?"

"No, but based on this one, and yet quite different."

He looks across the sea, thinks for a minute and begins. "A fish caught in a heron's beak was a cultivated soul. She knew her fables. She understood the necessity of both courage and caution. 'O Heron,' she began, 'I have long heard tales of the beauty of your voice. Will you grant my dying wish and allow me the privilege of hearing your song?' She thought she had phrased her request rather cleverly. Even if the heron refused to sing, he would have to open his beak to say 'Yes' or 'No.'

"But the heron just grunted (without opening his beak). He had never sung a song in his life and he didn't like music much.

"The fish tried again. 'O Most Rare and Refined Heron,' she said as sweetly as she could manage, 'I am gratified that I am to be a part of your repast. But alas, I have left the most exquisite part of my anatomy in the depths of the ocean. Allow me to return and fetch it for you.'

"The heron snorted without letting the fish go.

He hadn't understood a word she'd said.

"The fish was now desperate. There were no wells she could invite the heron to fall into, no snares in which she could entrap the heron, and no spells with which she could charm or disarm him. At her wits' end she tried a final, feeble lie. 'O Heron,' she cried. 'Spare me, and I will give you anything you want!'

"The heron was gratified. He had an answer that would shut her up.

"'O Fish,' he retorted, 'right now, what I want more than anything in the world is to eat you up.'

"It was a long sentence. The fish leapt out of his beak. 'Sometimes,' she muttered as she swam away, 'it's necessary to make a fable that fits the situation.'"

Androcles and I both applaud. Aesop looks pleased. "Don't you see, Sprite," he says, gently for him. "We are storytellers. We tell stories for the fun of it and that's how the stories proliferate."

"That's not all," I protest. "When things aren't right, we have to tell stories that say they aren't right!"

He sighs. "All right, Sprite. I'll try harder, but we can't lay down the law."

"So I have to go back to my own world?"

"Yes."

"And what will you do?"

"I will be free," Aesop replies.

"Free from what?"

He looks surprised, as though the answer should be obvious. "From you, Sprite. From your unreliable books and prescriptive fantasies. From your wanting to confine me and my work to a fixed, unalterable thing. We live in time, Sprite. Don't you understand? The dream mutates and shifts."

Then he takes my hand and hurls me back to my broken world.

After that I don't know what happens. Even the unreliable books are silent. The fables remain – some of them anyway – repeated, mutated, fizzing with energy.